HIGH PRAISE FOR
ROBERT J. RANDISI!

"[Randisi] doesn't waste a phrase or a plot turn. . . . His prose is supple and never flashy."
—*Publishers Weekly*

"A skilled, uncompromising writer, Randisi knows which buttons to press—and how to press them."
—John Lutz, author of *Single White Female*

"Randisi knows his stuff and brings it to life."
—*Preview Magazine*

"Randisi has a definite ability to construct a believable plot around his characters."
—*Booklist*

"This is the hard-boiled detective story as it ought to be: tough, fast, savvy, with a touch of sentiment, but without pretension and fake moralizing. Enjoy!"
—Dean Koontz on *No Exit From Brooklyn*

JACK—IN THE FLESH

"Don't move!" someone called out. "We only want the money."

There was a flurry of activity in the alley, much of it in the dark. Harker went down. He had either tripped or been struck, Stoker didn't know for sure. As Stoker turned to face the men who were charging him, suddenly there was another presence in the darkness. Stoker saw a glint of silver and a splash of red. Two men were down, as something wet struck Stoker on the hand and sleeve. He tried in vain to see who was attacking them, but could only make out a darkened figure. The third man tried to scream, but the sound caught in his throat and he fell to the ground with blood flowing from a gash in his neck. Someone with a knife and an uncanny ability with it had handled the three men with ease.

The fourth man watched the action with horror. Then he was seized in an iron grip and lifted off his feet from behind and pulled into the darkness.

"Who are you?" a voice asked Stoker.

Stoker still could not make anyone out in the shadows. The light shining on him kept his eyes from adjusting.

"I—my name is Bram Stoker."

"Why are you looking for me . . . ?"

Other *Leisure* books by Robert J. Randisi:

Thrillers:
BLOOD ON THE ARCH
IN THE SHADOW OF THE ARCH
THE SIXTH PHASE
ALONE WITH THE DEAD

Westerns:
MIRACLE OF THE JACAL
TARGETT
LEGEND
THE GHOST WITH BLUE EYES

CURTAINS OF BLOOD

ROBERT J. RANDISI

LEISURE BOOKS NEW YORK CITY

For Marthayn,
My Obsession

A LEISURE BOOK®

December 2002

Published by

Dorchester Publishing Co., Inc.
276 Fifth Avenue
New York, NY 10001

If you purchased this book without a cover you should be aware that this book is stolen property. It was reported as "unsold and destroyed" to the publisher and neither the author nor the publisher has received any payment for this "stripped book."

Copyright © 2002 by Robert J. Randisi

All rights reserved. No part of this book may be reproduced or transmitted in any form or by any electronic or mechanical means, including photocopying, recording or by any information storage and retrieval system, without the written permission of the publisher, except where permitted by law.

ISBN 0-8439-5068-4

The name "Leisure Books" and the stylized "L" with design are trademarks of Dorchester Publishing Co., Inc.

Printed in the United States of America.

Visit us on the web at www.dorchesterpub.com.

CURTAINS
OF BLOOD

"This series of crimes has not yet passed from the memory—a series of crimes which appear to have originated from the same source and which at the time created as much repugnance in people everywhere as the notorious murders of Jack the Ripper . . ."
　　—From Bram Stoker's introduction to the
　　　Islandic Edition of *Dracula*, 1901

Prologue

August 31, 1888

Jack took solace from and refuge in the dark.

He took sustenance from the blood of others.

He'd mucked up the first cut, the one to the throat, but there was nowt he could do about that. It had taken two tries to do the deed, sever the windpipe and the spinal cord, but it *had* done the job and extinguished the woman right and proper. A whore, she was, so who would miss her, and his point would be made, wouldn't it?

The next cut was made from the bottom of the ribs on the right side, then beneath the pelvis and to the left side. His strength, combined with the sharpness of the blade, made the task easy.

He stood and looked up and down Buck's Row. Like most of Whitechapel at this time of night, the riffraff who inhabited this godforsaken part of the city were indoors, minding their own affairs. It was dark, just a bit of a moon and far enough from any gaslights, so that he and his victim were well covered by a blanket of black. Satisfied that he would not be disturbed, he returned to his task.

His hands were covered with her blood, and he enjoyed the feel of it between his fingers—hot, tacky, almost like heated jam. Also, the smell of it, thick in the air, seemed to swirl around his head. He lifted one hand to his face, sniffed, then stuck out his tongue and tasted her. The heat of her blood in his mouth was thrilling. He smacked his lips and had to force himself to resist taking a second taste.

Again, back to the task at hand.

He lightly cut her stomach lining, exposing the entrails, all the while humming. Not a song, but a tuneless hum, the kind one isn't even aware of making while working at something one enjoys. Finally he jabbed viciously at her privates with the blade, just to give the authorities something extra to think about. He thought he was done, but he needed to survey the deed. He stood then, his eyes well accustomed to the dark, and studied the fruits of his labor. Bending, he lifted her skirt up higher, just for effect, then nodded, utterly satisfied with this night's work.

Part One

Dr. Jekyll, Mr. Hyde, and the Whitechapel Murders

Chapter One

From the back of the Lyceum Theater, Bram Stoker watched his friend, his idol, his employer, his Master, Henry Irving, transform brilliantly from the civilized *Dr. Jekyll* into the monstrous *Mr. Hyde.* As they had been doing every night since the play had begun its run, the audience gasped in amazement. Stoker reacted the same way. Irving's performances continued to take his breath away as much as they had twelve years earlier, when he was the theater critic of the *Evening Mail* in Dublin. Now, at forty-one, he was no less taken with the man's genius.

However, since managing the Lyceum Theater was part of his duties, he could not afford to spend

5

the time it would take to watch the entire performance. Once Irving made the first transformation, Stoker turned and left.

Strolling through the halls, he could smell the dinner that would be served immediately following the performance. Only honored guests and cast members were invited to the suite that once was the meeting place of the famed Beefsteakers Club. First formed in 1735, the Sublime Society of Beefsteaks boasted actors, playwrights, poets, and other honored guests as its members. It was Stoker who restored the Beefsteak Room to its former glory, he who chose the evening's diners and set out the place cards—which was the task he was on his way to do now.

As he entered the suite he admired the oak-paneled walls and high-beamed ceilings. It was while Irving was on a Mediterranean cruise that Stoker had the room redone, in order to surprise the actor upon his return. Irving had wholeheartedly approved of everything but insisted upon decorating the room. He did so with portraits of men he admired—David Garrick and William Charles Macready among them—and also Whistler's full-length portrait of Irving himself as Philip II, and his favorite leading lady, Ellen Terry, as Lady Macbeth. It was this painting that dominated the room.

The dining room was situated behind the stage, and invited guests gained access by way of a dusty old stairway that made it seem as if they were entering another age. The fact that the room was lined in old suits of armor lent credence to the fantasy.

Stoker walked through the room and entered the kitchen, which he'd had furnished with the most modern of equipment. The beef sizzled and spit on the new range. In the old days the white-coated cooks were in plain view of the diners, but now they worked in privacy.

"How are we coming?" Stoker asked Henry Boardman, the head chef.

"How do we ever come, guv?" the man asked. "Everything will be perfect."

Stoker knew that the beef would be accompanied by giant baked potatoes, onions and other vegetables. Since Henry Boardman had been put in charge of the meals, they had always been superb.

Stoker looked at the broad-shouldered man who appeared more like a dockworker than a chef. He touched his red beard and said, "Of course. Silly of me to ask."

Boardman chuckled good-naturedly. "But you ask every time . . . guv."

"So I do, Henry," Stoker said, "so I do. I will be in my office until dinner."

"Yes, sir."

Stoker's office was a small affair, but he'd had it furnished to his liking, all in dark wood and smooth surfaces. He was seated behind his desk, awaiting the end of the play, when there came a knock at the door.

"Come in."

The door opened and Joseph Harker entered. The young man, along with William Telbin and Hawes Craven, was one of the Lyceum's three scene painters. Harker was talented, but the thirty-three-year-old had been hired by Irving not because of his artistic ability, but rather in repayment of a favor. Harker's father had hired an eighteen-year-old Irving when they were both at the Edinburgh Royal Theater.

"Not watching the performance, Joseph?" Stoker asked.

"I was called away," Harker said.

"By what?"

"Someone came into the theater looking for you, Bram." It was soon after Harker was hired that Stoker convinced him not to call him *Mr. Stoker.* "When they couldn't find you, one of the ushers informed me of our visitors."

"Who?"

"Some policemen."

Stoker sat back in the chair and regarded Harker curiously.

"What would the police want with me?"

"Shall I show them in so you can ask them yourself?"

"By all means." He still had half an hour before the performance would end and guests began filing into the Beefsteak Suite.

Harker withdrew and returned with two men in

tow. One was Stoker's age, while the other one was younger, closer to Harker's age, perhaps even a few years less. The older man's mode of dress and his demeanor—not to mention his age—pointed him out as the one in authority.

"Mr. Stoker?" he asked, approaching the desk.

"I am Bram Stoker."

"My name is Chief Inspector Donald Swanson," the man said. "This is Sergeant Hobbs."

Stoker exchanged nods with Hobbs and shook hands with the chief inspector.

"What can I do for you, sir?" Stoker asked.

"I was actually here to see Mr. Irving," Swanson said, looking around. His eyes settled on Harker for a moment, then turned back to Stoker. "However, this gentleman informed me that he was on stage at the moment."

"Yes. We're doing *Dr. Jekyll and Mr. Hyde,*" Stoker said.

"I see. Then perhaps I could wait for him to finish?"

"He will be on stage for another thirty minutes or so," Stoker explained. "After that he dines with guests. Perhaps I could help you? I manage the theater." He was much more than the theater manager, but perhaps it was in this capacity he could help the policeman.

"You might actually be the one I should speak to, then, sir," Swanson said.

"Please," Stoker said, "have a seat."

Swanson sat in a chair across from Stoker. Harker remained standing to one side of the door, and Hobbs on the other.

"I'm afraid I am the bearer of bad news."

"What sort of bad news?"

"Have you heard that another woman was killed?"

"No," Stoker said. "Where?"

"Buck's Row, in Whitechapel."

"How many does that make?"

"Three."

"And the killer?"

Swanson shrugged.

"So he got away again?"

"Yes."

"Leaving not one clue?"

"We are investigating, sir."

Stoker frowned. "And your investigation has brought you to the Lyceum?"

Swanson looked unhappy. "I am here on direct orders from my superiors."

"To do what?"

"I'm afraid—it's to close you down."

"What?"

"You can't!" Harker said, aghast. "Close the Lyceum?"

"Well . . ." Swanson said, without turning to acknowledge Harker. When he spoke it was directly to Stoker. "Not the theater, so much as the performance."

"You want us to stop doing *Jekyll and Hyde?*"

10

"Not me—but that is essentially correct. You see, there are those who believe that this play might be . . . inciting the killer to do what he has been doing."

"This is just a story, Inspector," Stoker said, "a fiction, and a brilliant one at that, but staged strictly for entertainment. True, it's about one man's battle with another, darker personality inside him, but . . ."

Swanson spread his hands. "This Whitechapel killer may be having the same problem."

"He's a mad killer," Stoker said. "There can be no comparison."

"I've seen the play, Mr. Stoker," Swanson said. "Mr. Hyde is also a mad killer."

"Dr. Jekyll is not," Stoker said. "And it is he who is real . . . within the context of the play, of course."

"Well, perhaps the same is true of this killer," Swanson said, and then added, "within the context of real life."

Stoker was becoming agitated.

"But it's ridiculous to blame a man's crimes on . . . on a play!"

"Believe me," the inspector said, "I made the same argument. It fell on deaf ears. My superiors believe what they want to believe."

"Out of fear," Stoker said, "and ignorance."

"Exactly."

The sergeant shifted uncomfortably from one foot to the other. Hearing the inspector agree with

Stoker's assessment of both their superiors tested his loyalty.

"And these are the men who are trying to apprehend this madman?"

"As am I," Swanson said. "I am also trying to catch him, but my opinion on . . . on these matters has not been solicited."

"Well, you've delivered your news," Stoker said. "What happens if we do not comply?"

Swanson looked pained. "In that event I'm afraid the Lyceum would be shut down indefinitely. I would personally hate to see that happen, Mr. Stoker. My wife and I have spent many pleasant evenings here."

"You and your wife enjoy the theater?"

"Immensely," Swanson admitted. "Particularly Mr. Irving's performances."

Stoker regarded the inspector quizzically now. If he and his wife enjoyed Irving's performances, that meant the policeman knew in advance that a performance would be in process and Irving would be on stage now. Swanson had not had the heart to give the bad news directly to the actor.

"Inspector," Stoker said, "I would offer you and your wife free tickets to our next production, but I am unsure when that will be."

"Surely you can stage another play," Swanson said.

"I'm afraid it's a little more complicated than that, sir," Stoker said. "A lot of preparation goes into a production. And I fear Mr. Irving will be too upset to think about it for a while."

"I'm genuinely sorry, Mr. Stoker."

"I believe you, sir." Stoker took a deep breath and let it out slowly, stroking his beard as he did so. Then he nodded, as if he had come to some sort of decision. "Why don't you and your sergeant join us in the Beefsteak Room for dinner tonight?"

"Will you be telling Mr. Irving what's been decided?" the inspector asked.

"Oh, not until we've dined with our guests," Stoker said, "and perhaps not even until tomorrow. But where are my manners? Please, you and the good sergeant be our guests. Perhaps you might enlighten all of us about your investigation."

"Well," Swanson said, uncomfortably, "if it comes up."

"Sir?" Sergeant Hobbs spoke up.

"Yes, Sergeant?" Swanson did not turn to regard his sergeant.

"We really should be getting back to the station, guv."

"You'll be off duty soon, won't you, Sergeant?"

"Yes, sir."

"Then by all means return to the station and go on home from there." He waved a hand blindly at the man and said to Stoker, "I would be happy to join you for dinner, Mr. Stoker. Being invited into the Beefsteak Room is an honor."

"Excellent," Stoker said. "Joseph, would you have

them set another place at the table? And make it close to me."

"All right."

To Swanson, Stoker said, "I've actually been particularly interested in the case of the Whitechapel killer. I have many questions."

"Of course."

"Mr. Harker will show you the way."

"Won't you be coming?" the policeman asked, getting to his feet.

"Soon," Stoker assured him. "Very soon."

Once the two policemen had left with Joseph Harker, Stoker rose and walked to the window. He had chosen a room that overlooked the rear of the theater, on Burleigh Street, for his office, where he and Irving had a private entrance. He stood there staring out with hands clasped behind his back.

Of course he was aware of what had been going on in Whitechapel; some madman killing women, cutting them up, and he knew exactly how many there had been. In truth, he had been following the stories of these killings with great interest. There had been much discussion over breakfast with his wife, Florence, about the dangers to women walking alone at night, though he had not given the matter much thought. In point of fact, what time there was that was not taken up these days by his duties at the theater had been devoted to the book ruminating in his mind for years and lately demanding to be written. The actions of the Whitechapel killer had become very much a part of those ruminations. In fact, Florence had lately exhibited impatience with him whenever he began to discuss it. She was in favor of more genteel conversation at the kitchen table.

But while the murders interested him greatly as a writer, now the deaths had impacted not only on his life but on Henry Irving's as well. Not to mention theatergoers all over London. They had no choice but to accede to the *request* of the police and discontinue the run of *Dr. Jekyll and Mr. Hyde*—which would leave the remainder of the Lyceum's season in limbo.

Chapter Two

Stoker arrived at the Beefsteak Room in time for Irving's entrance. The actor always came to dinner in costume. However, it remained to be seen if he would attend as Dr. Jekyll or as Mr. Hyde. Stoker hoped for Jekyll, because Irving had a habit of remaining in character during dinner.

Dinner was taken by all at a long wooden table that dominated the center of the room. Irving always sat at the head, Stoker mid-table, in order to "direct traffic," if necessary. He usually placed some dignitary or other at the end of the table opposite Irving. Tonight that was his friend, Dr. Arthur Conan Doyle.

Though not yet thirty, Conan Doyle had already published extensively, with moderate success. His novella, *A Study in Scarlet,* introducing the consulting detective Sherlock Holmes and his companion, Dr. Watson, had appeared two years earlier in *Cornhill Magazine.* Stoker had enjoyed it very much, but due to its length the critics had largely ignored it. Stoker knew Conan Doyle had recently completed a novel entitled *Micah Clarke* but was having trouble finding a publisher. He was sure, however, that his friend was tenacious enough to overcome such a hurdle very soon. Indeed, even while trying to sell his novel he had completed another project, *The Mystery of Cloomb,* which had, for some reason, found a publisher fairly quickly. It was not, Stoker thought, Conan Doyle's best work. It lacked the energy and imagination of *A Study in Scarlet.*

Also present at the table, and holding court until Irving entered, was Lady Macbeth herself—the famous actress Ellen Terry, Oscar Wilde, and the former prime minister William Ewart Gladstone. Stoker shared an inexplicable affinity with Gladstone, and was fascinated by his odd avocation of attempting to "save" prostitutes as charitable work. The rest were actors, politicians, gentry, nearly twenty in all—seated at a table that could accommodate as many as thirty-six.

To Stoker's satisfaction Joseph Harker had managed to seat Inspector Swanson to his immediate left, and therefore closer to the head of the table. He was amused by the fact that the policeman's attention was apparently torn between

Terry's beauty and Wilde's bright, flowered waist-coat, white silk cravat and lilac-colored gloves.

In the old days of the Beefsteak Club, women were never allowed to attend, but Irving had long ago made allowances for Terry. It was left to her discretion whether or not she would dine with them on any given night.

"Bram, who is that stranger seated next to you?" Conan Doyle called from his end of the table. Leave it to the creator of Sherlock Holmes to exhibit curiosity about the newcomer at the table.

"Someone you will be especially interested in, Arthur," Stoker replied. "Inspector Swanson of the Metropolitan Police, meet Dr. Arthur Conan Doyle."

Suddenly, the battle for the inspector's attention was won by a third party, and he turned to face Conan Doyle.

"Mr. Doyle, this is indeed an honor," Swanson said. "Not only have I read and enjoyed *A Study in Scarlet*, but also *The Medical Casebook of Doctor Arthur Conan Doyle*."

"A book about me, but not penned by me," Conan Doyle pointed out to anyone listening, "but I am gratified by your comments, Inspector. It is indeed a compliment coming from a professional detective."

"Who's a detective?" the prime minister asked.

Since all other conversation at the table had stopped when the P.M. spoke, Stoker took the opportunity to introduce the inspector to the table at large.

"Swanson?" Gladstone repeated, frowning. "I know that name. Where do I know that name from?"

Before Swanson could answer for himself, Stoker said, "Inspector Swanson is the man in charge of investigating the Whitechapel murders."

"Of course. That's where I've heard your name," the former prime minister barked.

Swanson was giving Stoker a hard stare, feeling that he had been bamboozled, not being warned that the former prime minister would be present at dinner.

"Well, sir, I am not actually in charge as much as I am working under Commissioner Warren and Assistant Commissioner Anderson."

"Don't be so modest, man," Stoker said. "You are a chief inspector, are you not?"

"Indeed I am," Swanson said. "A chief inspector of Scotland Yard."

"Excellent!" the P.M. said loudly. "Perhaps you can fill us in on some details, then. There was another one last night, was there not?"

"Yes, sir."

"A prostitute?"

"We believe the victim to have been involved in prostitution, yes," Swanson said. He was suddenly craving the appearance of Henry Irving so that the attention would be diverted from him—but it was not all that unpleasant to have the unwavering stare of Ellen Terry upon him.

"But what of the killer?" Ellen Terry asked. "Don't you have any idea who he might be?"

"It is all under investigation, Miss Terry," Swanson said. "I assure you, we are following up every lead."

"But those poor women . . . slashed . . . ripped that way . . ." Ellen Terry said, shuddering. "It makes a woman afraid to go out on her own."

"Ellen," a young actor spoke up, "you needn't go out on your own, ever."

"And who is going to protect me from this fiend, Giles, you?" she asked.

"And why not?" the young man asked brazenly.

"Please, darling," Terry said, "aren't you the one who always says you're a lover and not a fighter? What would you do, dear, hug him to death?"

The young man's face reddened as the rest of the table laughed and he took sanctuary in a glass of port.

"Miss Terry," Oscar Wilde said, speaking for the first time, "I'm sure the inspector can tell you that this killer is certainly not targeting women of your station."

"No, indeed," Swanson said. "He certainly does seem intent on ridding the city of women of a, er, lower standing."

"Prostitutes," Wilde said.

"Primarily," Swanson added.

"The poor women," Gladstone said. "If they'd

only mended their ways, they might have saved their lives."

Ever the crusader, Stoker thought.

"Very possibly," the policeman replied.

At that moment the door opened and the imposing figure of Henry Irving entered. He had chosen to remain in his stage persona as Dr. Jekyll tonight—not Hyde. For this Stoker gave silent thanks.

He greeted the table at large, then sat and addressed the prime minister and Oscar Wilde individually. Then he peered down at the end of the table and asked, "Is that you, Doyle?" At the same time he lifted Terry's hand to his lips and kissed it. She was always seated to his immediate left.

"In the flesh." Conan Doyle lifted his glass. "Marvelous performance, as usual, Henry—both of them."

Irving lifted his own glass. "Would you expect anything less?"

"Never," Conan Doyle said with a laugh.

"What was the subject of the conversation when I walked in?" Irving asked. "You all looked so . . . so somber."

"Those ghastly Whitechapel murders, dear friend," Oscar Wilde answered.

"My God," Irving said, "don't we get enough of that from the newspapers?"

"But it isn't often you have one of the detectives investigating the case sitting at your own table," Ellen Terry said.

"Eh? Who's that?" Irving asked, looking around

the table. Finally he located the unfamiliar guest seated next to Stoker.

"Bram?"

"This is Inspector Swanson, guv," Stoker said. "Of Scotland Yard. He is working on the murders."

"Inspector," Irving said. "Welcome to the table."

"Thank you, sir."

"The inspector and his wife are great fans of yours."

"Indeed? Well, fans are always welcome. Did you see the performance tonight?"

"Uh, no, I didn't," the inspector said awkwardly.

"Well, then, you must come. I'll have Bram leave tickets at the box office for you. Just pick them up any night."

"I, uh . . . thank you, very much." The policeman felt particularly awkward.

"So, if you did not come to the theater to see the play tonight, why are you here?" Irving frowned. "Don't tell me you came on official business."

Stoker, having anticipated that Irving's curiosity would cause him to ask this question, had already waved to the headwaiter to begin serving dinner. Before Swanson could attempt a reply the kitchen doors opened and waiters appeared with their trays.

"Ah," Stoker announced, "dinner is served."

Conversation was abandoned while plates bearing great hunks of beef and heaps of vegetables were served. Crystal glasses were refilled with wine. However, once dinner was served and the waiters had withdrawn, Irving stood and raised his glass.

Tall and almost painfully gaunt, he seemed to tower over the table. His guests remained seated but raised their glasses as well. Swanson looked around, then glanced at Stoker, who nodded. The policeman correctly assumed this was a ritual and followed suit.

"Ladies and gentlemen," Henry Irving said, " 'to the general joy o' th' whole table.' "

The quote from *Macbeth* was everyone's signal to begin eating.

Chapter Three

During dinner Stoker turned the conversation with Inspector Swanson more toward the killer than the actual murders. He took this as an opportunity to do some very intimate research into the mind of the killer, through that of the policeman pursuing him. Stoker noticed, however, how intently the inspector's attentions were focused on Henry Irving.

Over the second course of toasted cheese and port, Swanson became aware that while he was watching Irving, Stoker was watching him.

"He's quite amazing, isn't he?" the detective asked.

"Yes, he is," Stoker said, "in many ways, but to which of those are you referring?"

"The way he stays in character," Swanson said.

"Does he ever come to dinner as Mr. Hyde, and how do guests tolerate him then?"

"He's entertaining."

"But the character of Mr. Hyde . . ."

"Well, Inspector," Stoker said, "he doesn't kill anyone."

"No, of course not. And what about when he leaves the theater to return home?"

"What about it?"

"Well . . . does he remain in character, then?"

Stoker sat back in his chair and regarded the inspector quizzically. He was extremely happy now that Irving had not chosen to come to the table as Mr. Hyde. He had done so the night before and acted in an almost scandalous manner. If there had been strangers present, they would have been appalled by his behavior. Truth be told, Stoker had not found the evening pleasant at all. Lately he'd been thinking Irving's immersion into the character of Hyde was . . . disturbing. As he studied Swanson it suddenly hit him.

"This can't be," he said finally.

"What can't be?"

"I was wondering why they would send a man of your stature here to close us down," Stoker said. "Now I see."

"Do you?"

Stoker shook his head in wonder. "Are you so desperate to stop these murders that you'd actually suspect Henry Irving?"

Swanson regarded Stoker silently for a few moments. "We suspect everyone at this point, Mr. Stoker."

"You honestly believe that if Irving happens to leave the theater in character—in the character of Mr. Hyde—he goes out and kills lowborn women? Prostitutes?"

To his credit, the inspector looked embarrassed.

"It is just one hypothesis . . . and not mine. . . ."

"Why not, then, suspect Mr. Gladstone?"

Swanson looked at Stoker as if he were crazy.

"The prime minister? Are you mad?"

"Why not?" Stoker asked. "You yourself heard the way he spoke about prostitutes."

"He—he said he wanted to save them."

"And couldn't he do that by killing them?"

For just a moment the inspector seemed to consider Stoker's suggestion, then shook his head. "It's . . . it's ridiculous. You can't be serious."

"Well, then, you can't be serious about suspecting Henry Irving," Stoker said.

"I'm just doing my job, Mr. Stoker," Swanson said. "I'm investigating every possibility."

"Henry Irving being the Whitechapel madman is not a possibility, Inspector," Stoker argued. "Believe me."

When dinner was over the inspector thanked Stoker for the invitation and the two men shook hands. Each had his own reasons for both offering and accepting the invitation, but now neither was sure they had gotten what he was looking for. As Swanson walked out Oscar Wilde approached Stoker.

Wilde was fresh from a recent triumph. His poem "Ravenna" had won the prestigious Newdigate Prize. Early in their friendship the two had vied for the affection of Stoker's wife, Florence. Stoker had won that battle in December of 1878, but in 1884 Wilde himself had married Constance Lloyd. No bad feelings had lingered concerning their old rivalry, and the two were great friends. Wilde became a staple at the Lyceum, often holding court from his box.

"What were you and the inspector discussing so earnestly?" Wilde asked.

Stoker regarded his friend gravely for a moment, unsure whether or not he should confide in him.

"Oh, come now," Wilde prompted. "If it's something you must think about first, you can't keep it from me."

Stoker put his arm around Wilde's shoulders and drew him aside. He confided the content of his conversation with Inspector Swanson, and was surprised when Wilde did not laugh out loud. In fact, Wilde shocked him with his next statement.

"That is not a bad hypothesis, you know."

"What?" Stoker asked. "You're as mad as he is if you think Henry could—"

"Oh, not Henry, you daft bugger!" Wilde said, cutting his friend short. "Gladstone."

"I was not serious when I suggested—"

"But consider it," Wilde said. "The old boy has a

bee in his bonnet about whores, doesn't he?"

"It's nothing," Stoker said, "a harmless . . . well, hobby." He was at a loss for a better word.

"A hobby?" Wilde asked, and now he did laugh. "Accosting prostitutes on the street?"

"Trying to save them."

"And wouldn't killing them be saving them?" Wilde asked, echoing Stoker's own insincere argument to Swanson.

"Oscar, you can't be serious!"

"What can't he be serious about?" a voice asked.

They turned and found Conan Doyle standing behind them.

"Come, come, gentlemen," Conan Doyle said, "no secrets from a fellow scribe. One for all, and all that."

"Doyle, I can't—" Stoker began, but Wilde cut him off and spilled the beans to Conan Doyle about their discussion.

"Gladstone?" he said, stroking his chin. "Hmm . . . as an alternative to Henry?"

"It's preposterous," Stoker said, "either way. I'm sorry I ever brought it up." He glared at Oscar Wilde, who smiled back at him with unrestrained glee. "Oh, you're enjoying this too much!"

"Well," Conan Doyle said thoughtfully, "there is a case to be made either way."

"What?" Stoker was appalled.

"Henry does tend to stay in character too long sometimes," Conan Doyle said.

"But—"

"And Gladstone," the physician went on, "well . . . he does go on and on about prostitutes."

"You're both mad!" Stoker said. "I'm surrounded by madmen."

"Fancy a pint?" Wilde asked Conan Doyle.

"Just one," the other said, "and then I must return home."

"Bram?"

"I can't," Stoker said. "I—there's something I must speak to Henry about."

"More news?" Wilde asked excitedly.

"Never mind," Stoker said. "Off you both go to the nearest pub, and take your mad suspicions with you."

"We're going," Wilde said, "we're going. Come, Doyle. Perhaps over a pint your keen detective's mind can come up with an alternate solution to these crimes."

"Good night, Bram," Conan Doyle said.

Stoker waved them away, then turned to locate Henry Irving among the remainder of the milling guests. He found him in a corner, a cadaverous Dr. Jekyll deep in conversation with the prime minister, William Gladstone. For a moment he regarded the two men critically, wondering if it were possible—and then he shook his head to dispel such thoughts. Suspecting either of them was as ludicrous as suspecting himself. What would Inspector Swanson think if he knew that Stoker's new book, which was beginning to take up all his thoughts during his hours away from the Lyceum, might have to do with a creature even more vile than the Whitechapel madman?

Chapter Four

Stoker waited for Irving to finish his conversation with Gladstone before approaching them. He shook hands with the prime minister and bade him good night.

"Interesting dinner," Irving said. "Why did you bring that policeman, Bram?"

"I didn't bring him, guv," Stoker said. "He came on his own."

"Invited himself to dinner?"

"No," Stoker said, amending his statement. "I extended the invitation only after he came on a police matter."

"And what was that?"

"Something we have to talk about."

Henry Irving looked around the room. He never

Robert J. Randisi

left the suite until all his guests had gone. Now all
that remained were the waiters, cleaning away de-
bris from the long table.

"Let's go to my dressing room, then," Irving said.
"We can talk while I rid myself of Dr. Jekyll."

Stoker followed Irving to his dressing room,
which was larger than his own office. That was all
right with him, though. The Lyceum existed because of Henry Irving's vision, and his talent. That
meant he was entitled to anything he wanted. Stoker was well satisfied with his own small office.

He closed the door while Irving removed Dr. Jekyll's jacket and handed it to his dresser, Walter Collinson. Collinson was a small, wiry, bespectacled
man who was Irving's closest confidant—closer
even than Stoker, who idolized the actor. Stoker,
however, understood the long history between the
two men and had long ago decided that jealousy
was not an option. In one corner of the room Irving's dog, Fussie, looked at them from his basket.
To Stoker he hardly resembled a dog, just a ball of
hair from which beady little eyes stared, and a tiny
pink tongue protruded. To Irving, however, the animal was a prized possession, closer to him than
even the dresser.

Collinson hung the garment on a rack alongside
other jackets and costumes while Irving sat down
in front of his makeup mirror. The consummate
professional, he always took care of his own
makeup.

"What's on your mind, Bram?"

"It's not good, chief." Stoker called Irving "guv" or "chief," but the latter was a privilege only he was privy to.

Irving regarded him, using the mirror. "It never is when you get that look. The longer it takes you to tell me, the worse it will be—or is it already as bad as it can get?"

Stoker hesitated, then said, "The inspector was here to tell us the police are closing us down."

Irving turned, one Jekyll eyebrow on and one off, giving him a comically quizzical appearance.

"The theater?" Collinson asked, his voice quavering slightly.

"Jekyll and Hyde," Stoker said. "They're closing down the production."

"Oh, my," the dresser said.

"Why?" Irving asked stiffly, all good humor gone.

"Because of the Whitechapel murders. They believe that your performance as Mr. Hyde may be inciting the maniac to . . . to kill more women."

Irving stared at Stoker for a few moments, then turned back to the mirror and peeled off the other eyebrow.

"They flatter me . . . the fools!"

"A madman needs no impetus to kill," Collinson said with distaste, "especially not from the theater."

"Indeed," Irving agreed.

Although he'd never seen Irving overreact, Stoker was surprised at the man's calm demeanor.

"Did you hear what I said, guv?"

"I heard," Irving said, "and I understood."

"So what are we supposed to do?"

Irving started wiping makeup from his face.

"What will happen if we do not comply?"

"They will close the theater."

"Well, then, they don't leave us much choice, do they?"

"Henry—"

"Bram—" Irving said, and waved away any further protestations.

"Shall I inform the cast, then?" Stoker asked.

"Gather them in the theater tomorrow," Irving said. "I will tell them myself."

"And then what?"

Again, Irving used the mirror to lock eyes with Stoker.

"We will have to find another play to do."

"That will take some time."

"Perhaps not," Irving said. "Perhaps it's time for the bloody play."

"*Macbeth*? But . . . the preparation."

"Ellen is already here," Irving said, "and the others know the play."

"Still, we will need other actors, other actresses, new scenes—"

"Talk to Joseph, Hawes and William." He was referring to Harker, Craven and Telbin, the trio of scene painters the Lyceum used. "Get them started."

"Very well. If you don't mind me saying so, chief, you are taking this extremely well."

Irving threw down the cotton rag he had been

holding and whirled about to face Stoker. The sudden movement startled Collinson, who gasped, and Fussie, who yipped. Irving, however, maintained his composure.

"What would you have me do, Bram?" Irving asked. "Cry, wail, rend my clothes? Allow them to close us down completely by attempting to defy them?"

"We could talk to Gladstone," Stoker said. "He could possibly make them—"

"No." Irving shook his head. "I won't ask him to do that."

"Why not?"

"Because he might not help us. Then I would have to ask him why, and I fear I would not like his answer. I might even lose respect for him because of it."

"I could ask him. He and I get along—"

"No," Irving said, cutting him off. "We'll stop doing *Jekyll and Hyde,* as they demand. Maybe they're right." He turned to look at himself closely in the mirror. "Maybe I am so good in the role of Hyde that I *am* having an effect on this man."

Stoker opened his mouth to say something and then stopped. A thought occurred to him, but he didn't want to voice it, at least not yet. He looked to Collinson for help, but none was forthcoming. Whatever the dresser had to say about the matter would be said to his master in private, never in front of Stoker.

"I am going to finish up here and then go home,"

Irving said. "I suggest you do the same. You can contact everyone tomorrow morning, have them here in the evening. And put a sign out in the box office."

"We will have to refund a lot of money," Stoker said. "It's going to hurt our finances."

"We'll recover," Irving said. "Perhaps the ticket holders will simply wait for *Macbeth.*"

"Henry—"

"We can deal with all of this tomorrow, Bram," Irving said wearily. "I'm tired. I don't want to think about it tonight."

"All right, chief," Stoker said. "I'll lock up and go home."

"Fine," Irving said. "Check the kitchen, too. Make sure they've turned off that newfangled oven of yours."

"All right."

Stoker turned and took hold of the doorknob.

"Bram?"

"Yes, guv?"

Irving turned to look at him. "Nothing. I'll see you in the morning."

" 'Night, guv."

Stoker left the room, closing the door behind him. He didn't know what Irving was going to say, or why he changed his mind. He was sure of one thing, though. Henry Irving knew that his performance as Mr. Hyde had nothing to do with the murders. He knew as well as Stoker did that the first murder was months ago, before they had even started performing *Dr. Jekyll and Mr. Hyde*. Why, then, had he so easily conceded the point as possible?

Chapter Five

During the time Bram and Florence Stoker had lived on Cheyne Walk in Chelsea he had acquired the habit of taking the Cadogan Ferry across the Thames each day to get to the Lyceum, on Wellington Street in London. After they had moved—at Florence's insistence—to 17 St. Leonard's Terrace—still in Chelsea, but according to her a much more desirable location—Stoker continued to take the ferry, even though it was now a brisk ten-minute walk away.

Florence had insisted they move because one day, during his ferry ride, Stoker had spotted a man who had jumped into the Thames to attempt suicide. Immediately he tore off his coat and vest and jumped into the water after the poor wretch. He did, indeed, manage to keep the man afloat until a rescue boat arrived. He then had the man brought to his home on Cheyne Walk, where he ordered the man be laid upon his dining room table. He tried to revive the poor bugger by using a mouth-to-mouth technique, but his attempts failed and the fellow died. When Florence arrived home to find a dead stranger on her table she was appalled. Stoker received a bronze medal from the Royal Humane Society, and much publicity as a hero, but from that day on Florence hated the Cheyne Walk address.

On this particular evening Stoker did not walk briskly from the ferry to St. Leonard's Terrace, but took his time. He had many things on his mind, not the least of which was Henry Irving's meek acquiescence to the order from the police to discontinue performing *Dr. Jekyll and Mr. Hyde*. Certainly there were favors that might have been called in, arms twisted, even bribes paid to assure that the play continued, but Irving had suggested none of that.

Stoker also despaired for a city that would blame a play, a fictional story, for the actions of a madman.

And lastly, now that the actions of the Whitechapel killer had invaded his own life, he found the already growing fascination concerning both the murders and the man who had committed them increasing even more. Being able to talk with Inspector Swanson about it was a rare opportunity. He had wondered all along what sort of man could perpetrate such crimes against those poor women. Lowborn or not, they did not deserve such treat-

ment, such ends. The pain involved must have been
. . . excruciating.

He had asked Swanson some of the questions
that had been going about in his head all these
weeks. Was it possible that the killer reveled in the
pain of his victims even more than the actual killing
itself? And what of the blood? Copious amounts of
it, according to the accounts he had read and heard.
Swanson, though, was not very forthcoming with
information about the killer. Stoker was wondering
how else he could do the research he needed.

There were many nights—most of them, in fact—
when Florence did not wait up for him. She knew
that when he was dining with Irving he often returned home late. Tonight, however, it was as if she
knew he wanted to talk to her. When he entered the
house she set aside her knitting, rose from her chair
and went to him.

"My dear," he said, embracing her, hugging her
to his burly chest. She buried her face in his neck,
in the bushiness of his red beard.

"Bram," she said, "you're trembling."

"Am I?"

"It's a warm night . . ."

"Oh, I'm not cold, love," he said, holding her at
arm's length so he could look at her. "I'm . . . angry,
and confused."

"By what?"

"Get us both a brandy while I change," he said,
"and I will tell you."

He went to their bedroom, undressed, donned his dressing gown and returned to the parlor to accept the glass she offered.

Florence listened intently to Stoker as he explained everything that had occurred that night. When he was finished he refilled their brandy glasses, handed hers back to her and sat down on the sofa with her again.

"But surely this is madness," she said finally.

"Well, yes . . ."

"No, I mean from head to toe," she said. "It may be a fact that we do have a madman loose in the city, but to think a play would incite him to murder is mad, and equally insane is suspecting either Henry Irving or the P.M."

"Well," Stoker said meekly, "that last was my idea, but it was only to illustrate to the inspector how daft I thought he and his superiors were being."

"That was perhaps the least mad suggestion of all."

"Now you're sounding like Oscar!"

"Think about it," Florence said, "William Gladstone is fascinated by prostitutes."

"He likes to save them, not *kill* them." Stoker's tone was almost desperate. Could no one see the point?

"No matter," Florence insisted. "The fact is, they fascinate him, which in my book makes him a more likely suspect than your Henry."

"That may be so," Stoker said after a while, "but the reality is, neither of them did it."

"The reality, my love," Florence said, rising and placing a hand on his arm, "is that you *believe* neither of them is guilty."

"And you don't?"

"I don't know it for a fact, any more than you do. That is all I am saying. Are you coming to bed?"

"Soon," he said absently. "I still have a lot of thinking to do."

"About a new book, or about . . . all this?"

Evading the question, he said, "I would only toss and turn and keep you awake. Go on to bed and I shall be there shortly."

Florence knew that her definition of *shortly* greatly differed from that of her husband. She bent to kiss his lips. "Don't stay awake too long, my love."

"I won't," he said, taking her hand in his and squeezing it, "I promise. Good night."

"Good night." She tapped his glass. "And not too much brandy."

After she had gone he sneaked just a bit more brandy and then took it to his study with him. When he had thinking to do—no matter the subject—he liked to be surrounded by his books. He lit his lamp, turned it up just a bit, then sat behind his desk. He took a sip of brandy and then sat back in his chair and closed his eyes.

To simply stop performing *Jekyll and Hyde* and begin putting together a cast for *Macbeth* was not acceptable to him. As manager of the Lyceum, it was simply too costly. As an artist himself, it was almost a sacrilege.

He couldn't help but wonder how seriously the police were looking for this Whitechapel killer if they were prepared to suspect someone of the stature of Henry Irving. Or perhaps they were simply so baffled they were grasping at straws. If he were the one to find the killer he would be able to learn about the man, and the dark forces that drove him. Robert Louis Stevenson's *Dr. Jekyll and Mr. Hyde* had fascinated Stoker as a book, and he had persuaded Irving to do it as a play. Seeing Irving perform night after night, he couldn't help but wonder if the great actor wasn't tapping into his own inner darkness in order to play the mad Mr. Hyde so convincingly.

He wondered if what he should do was go to Whitechapel and walk in the footsteps of the killer. Perhaps it would help him with his research, and he might even find out something useful to the police in catching him. Suddenly he sat up with a start, realizing that he had just set himself the task of retracing the killer's steps. To accomplish it, however—or to even attempt it—he would need the help of someone to whom deductive reasoning came as second nature. Someone whose curiosity might be as great as his own.

He knew just the man.

Chapter Six

September 2, 1888

When Stoker returned to the Lyceum the next day he had to unlock the front door to enter. That told him that no one else—Irving or Collinson, the only other men with keys—were there yet. He went to his office and hung up his coat. Florence had gotten up with him to make tea that morning, and while they talked a bit over breakfast he decided against telling her about his decision to go to Whitechapel. She would have said it was just one more mad decision being made—and she would have been right. He thought it all over again during his ten-minute walk to the ferry and the ride across the Thames. By the time he reached the front of the theater he was still convinced that this was the only thing he could do. It would be invaluable to his research, and it might also help save the Lyceum's season. Perhaps someone would tell him something they wouldn't tell the police.

Still, he had to go through the motions of calling together cast and crew for *Macbeth*. But first he had to summon the *Dr. Jekyll and Mr. Hyde* cast so Irving could break the bad news to them.

He had several young assistants who worked at the Lyceum, running the most menial of errands just to be "in the theater." When they arrived he would dispatch them to the homes and hotels of the cast members. Before that, however, he had to send a runner to one special person's home to arrange a meeting.

The cast was set to meet at three. At one that afternoon Stoker was sitting in the Black Bull, a nearby pub where both theatrical and literary types gathered. He was talking to the man he hoped would help him find the Whitechapel killer.

"You're mad," Conan Doyle said. "Utterly and completely mad."

"Are you saying it can't be done?"

"The police have had four months to work on this, Bram," Conan Doyle said. "What makes you think you can solve it in a fraction of that time?"

"You."

"Me . . . what do you mean, me?"

"I'd like you to help me."

Conan Doyle sat back, leaning away from the pint on the table before him as if he thought just being near it would cause him to do something rash.

"Is that why you asked me here?"

"I don't know the first thing about running an investigation," Stoker reasoned.

"And I do?"

"Come on," Stoker said. "You created Sherlock Holmes."

"And that qualifies me to conduct investigations?" Doyle asked. "That's like me asking my friend James Barrie to show me how to fly simply because he's written about fairies."

"Doyle, you can't tell me—"

"I'm a physician and a writer," Conan Doyle said, "not a detective."

He picked up his pint and took a defiant drink.

"All right," Stoker said after a few moments, "then don't tell me what you would do, tell me what Holmes would do, or your mentor, Dr. Bell."

Conan Doyle stared at Stoker for a moment, then set down his pint and leaned back again.

"You've been following these cases," Stoker said. "I know you, Doyle. You could not resist reading the newspaper accounts."

"Yes," Conan Doyle admitted, "I have been following them. . . ."

"And you've probably thought of some things the police haven't done."

"No."

"What do you mean, no? Surely you have a theory."

"Well, yes, of course I have a theory, but—"

"Then that's all I ask of you," Stoker said, cutting his friend off. "Share it with me."

Conan Doyle regarded his friend for a short time. "You are truly serious about this?"

"Deadly."

The other man shook his head. "I think you are heading for disaster, Stoker. You are not equipped to deal with a killer of this . . . well, you're not equipped to deal with any killer."

"I don't want to capture him," Stoker said. He did not want to speak to Conan Doyle about his research. "I want to find out who he is and tell the police. I want them to arrest him, and then let us get on with our performance of *Jekyll and Hyde*."

"Your motives are good, Bram," said Conan Doyle, "but I think your action ill advised."

"Nevertheless, will you help me?"

"You will pursue this whether I help or not, won't you?" Conan Doyle asked with a sigh.

"Yes."

"Very well," the doctor said. "Logic is the key. If you pursue this logically you might actually achieve your goal."

"And what does logic dictate I do?"

"This could be time consuming."

"Doyle—"

"All right," the other man said, holding up one hand. "First, go to the scenes of the murders."

"All of them?"

"I told you it would take time—"

"Yes, yes, all right," Stoker said, "go on, then."

"Go to the scenes of the murders and see what you can find out. Also, see if you feel anything."

"What do you mean, *feel?*"

"Use your instincts, man," Conan Doyle said. "We all have them. They're natural. Open yourself up to them. Let yourself feel. Do you understand?"

"I think so. Shall I go in the day or night?"

"Both," Conan Doyle said. "It could be important to see them at the same time as they took place, but there will be more people for you to talk with during the day."

"All right, day and night. Go on." Stoker spoke as if he were taking notes, but he was simply committing everything Conan Doyle said to memory.

"Then you must learn all you can about the victims."

"How many have there been? Isn't it three?"

"Yes, three. Speak to their landlords, their friends . . . their pimps, if you can. You cannot find out too much, Stoker. Remember that."

"Shall I talk to the police? Find out what they know?"

"No," Conan Doyle said, "that is precisely what you must not do. Don't find out what they know, but gather your own information."

"All right," Stoker said. "Anything else?"

"Frequent the same places these types of people frequent," Conan Doyle said.

"Bawdy houses, you mean?"

"Pubs, bawdy houses, rooming houses, wherever these women lived or, if they were indeed prostitutes, where they plied their trade."

"And after I've done all that?"

"Put all your information together," Conan Doyle said, "and see what it tells you."

"When I have it all together, would you consent to look at it with me?"

"Consent?" Conan Doyle said with a surprised look. "Why, my good man, I insist upon it."

"So you are curious about all this."

"Yes, indeed," Conan Doyle said. "I never said I wasn't."

"Then why were you reluctant to help me?"

"I told you," the other man said. "I don't think you're up to it, Stoker. You're a big man, yes, a strong one, but we're talking about a mad killer."

"Perhaps I should . . . bring someone to help me, then."

"Like who? A bodyguard?"

"No," Stoker said. "A Watson of my own."

"Don't look at me," Conan Doyle said immediately. "I will look at the information after you've gathered it, but I won't run around in dark alleys and bawdy houses to find it. Unlike you, I know my physical limitations. I would not want to go up against this man in a dark Whitechapel alley."

"But we would be together."

"I have little confidence in either of our physical abilities to fend off such a man." Conan Doyle spoke with finality. "I'm afraid, Stoker, you'll have to find your Watson elsewhere."

Chapter Seven

Stoker returned to the Lyceum before the first of the cast members began to arrive. Joseph Harker, however, was already waiting for him in his office.

"Bram," he said, as Stoker entered, "what is going on?"

Stoker closed the door and turned to face the younger man.

"How much do you know, Joseph?"

"Nothing. This morning I was told to start thinking about sets for *Macbeth*. Bram . . . what about *Jekyll and Hyde?*"

Stoker moved behind his desk and sat down.

"You heard what the inspector said yesterday, Joseph," Stoker said. "*Jekyll and Hyde* is no more."

"I heard about that, but I didn't think Mr. Irving would allow it to happen."

"Well, he has. He wants us to begin preparing to put on *Macbeth*."

"But that will take time," Harker said. "What will we do until then?"

"Close down."

"But . . . that will cost us a fortune."

"Nothing we can do, Joseph." Stoker hadn't intended to take anyone else into his confidence. However, he *did* need a Watson.

"Joseph . . . sit down, will you? I have something I want to talk to you about."

Ten minutes later Harker sat stunned.

"What I have planned will be dangerous," Stoker said.

"Having the theater go out of business will be dangerous also," Harker said. "It will leave me without a job, or a career."

"That's nonsense. You can get work in any theater."

"I want to work at the Lyceum."

"Well, then, there seems to be only one way to do that," Stoker said. "I need to find out who is killing women in Whitechapel." Once again, as with Conan Doyle, Stoker did not speak to Harker of his research. He had not even spoken to Florence about the book he was planning.

"*We* need to find out," Harker corrected him. "How do we start?"

"Doyle told me one other thing before we parted company at the pub."

"What was that?"

"He thinks the police may know more than they are telling the public."

"Conan Doyle thinks they have some evidence?"

"More than that," Stoker said, folding his hands on top of his desk. "He thinks they may already know who the killer is."

When Stoker and Harker entered the theater from the back, Ellen Terry and the rest of the cast were sitting in the audience. The actors turned and watched the two men walk down the aisle.

"What is happening, Bram?" Ellen Terry asked. "What's this all about?"

"We all want to know that," the young actor, Giles Harris, added.

"Henry wants to tell you himself," Stoker said. "He'll be out shortly."

She looked at Harker, who simply shrugged his shoulders. As Stoker's confidant and assistant now, he had agreed to back whatever action his boss took.

Giles stood and faced Stoker.

"Is this some kind of game, Stoker?" he demanded. "We all have things to do before tonight's performance."

According to Stoker's instructions, there were to be no PERFORMANCE CANCELED bills posted outside the theater until all the actors were inside.

57

"There will be no performance tonight," Stoker said, speaking to them all.

"No performance?" Ellen Terry asked.

"What are you talking about?" Giles asked loudly. "What's going on? We have a right to know."

Suddenly they heard footsteps, and all turned. Henry Irving stood center stage, staring down at them. He was dressed simply in trousers and a white shirt that was open at the collar. Even in casual attire, however, he commanded attention.

"Sit down, Giles," he said.

"But—"

"Sit!"

Giles sat quickly, and Irving had the attention of everyone in the theater.

"Bram is quite right," Irving began. "There will not be a performance of *Dr. Jekyll and Mr. Hyde* tonight, or any other night in the foreseeable future."

The actors exchanged glances but remained silent, except for Ellen Terry.

"Can we ask why, Henry?"

"I fully intended to tell you why, my love." Irving launched into an explanation of the true purpose of Inspector Swanson's visit the night before. He explained about Stoker's conversation with the policeman, and then the one they had in Irving's dressing room after dinner.

"You mean the man ate with us, knowing full well

he was closing us down?" one of the older actors asked. "That's . . . rude!"

"He was doing his job," Irving said. "The man is investigating a series of grisly murders. I don't believe one can hold him accountable for what one perceives is bad form."

"But Henry—" Ellen Terry started.

"Courage, my dear," Irving said, cutting her off. "The police have merely closed our performance of *Jekyll and Hyde*. They have not closed the theater."

"What do you propose to do, then?" she asked.

"My love," he asked, "how long has it been since you last played Lady Macbeth?"

Chapter Eight

The actors filed out, muttering among themselves. Some of them had never done *Macbeth* and weren't sure they were to be included. Others knew they would have smaller roles in the Shakespeare play. Irving took it upon himself to console Ellen Terry, which Stoker saw little or no reason for. Her role as Lady Macbeth would certainly afford her more opportunity to cover herself with accolades than her part in *Jekyll and Hyde* ever could have.

After they had all gone, Stoker and Harker were alone in the theater.

"That did not necessarily go well," Harker said.

"No matter," Stoker replied. "If we are successful, we will be able to go back to *Jekyll and Hyde*.

"What shall we do first?"

Stoker sat down in one of the theater seats and put up his feet on the back of another. He had not slept well, and his eyes were feeling heavy. He had actually dozed off on the ferry that morning.

"Joseph, why don't you go and research the murders? Get us all the information you can so we can study it. Names, locations, how each woman was killed."

"Where shall I go for all that? The police?"

"No, no, I don't want the inspector knowing what we're up to. And he probably wouldn't give it to you, anyway. Go to the tabloids. Go to the library and look at past copies of *The Times*."

"All right," Harker responded. "And what will you be doing while I'm researching?"

"I want to talk to Henry again. Maybe he's changed his mind about *Macbeth* now that he's had time to think things over."

"Where shall we meet?"

"Right here," Stoker said. "I'll be in my office until late this evening. If we do end up doing *Macbeth*, there's lots of work to be done."

"And sets to be painted."

"Don't worry," Stoker said. "You'll have time for that as well."

Harker did not seem convinced, but he did want to be part of Stoker's investigation.

"I'll see you this evening, then. Ta."

Stoker waved, and as Harker left he made a steeple of his fingers and studied them. He sat that way for a time, then rose and walked backstage, hoping to find Irving in his dressing room.

As Stoker approached, Irving's dressing room door opened and Collinson came out. They almost collided before the older man noticed he was there.

"Oh, Stoker." The man seemed frazzled, carrying a bundle of clothes in his arms. They appeared to be some of Irving's stage attire.

"Walter," Stoker said. "Is the chief inside?"

"Wha—no, he's not."

"Where did he go, then?"

"He and Miss Terry went for a drink," the dresser said. "She was terribly disappointed about the run of the play being canceled."

"Was she?"

"Yes, very disappointed."

"What about Henry, Walter?"

"I don't know—what do you mean?"

"Isn't he disappointed?"

"Well, yes, of course."

"Then why isn't he protesting it?"

Collinson hesitated, then said, "I have to go."

"What are those?"

"His clothes."

"What's that stain?"

"I—just have to get them washed," Collinson said. "I really must go."

"What's going on, Walter?" Stoker asked. "Why isn't Henry more upset about the play?"

"Why don't you ask him?"

"I did ask him, remember? Last night. You were there."

"Then he answered you," Collinson said. "He doesn't want them to close the whole theater down. And you . . . you should do what he asks of you."

"I always do, Walter . . . don't you? Don't we all do what Henry wants?"

"Of course. It's his theater, after all."

"Yes, it is," Stoker said. "Thank you for reminding me of that."

"I really must go," Collinson said, and hurried off down the hall and out of sight. Stoker wondered what had passed between Irving and his dresser after he left the dressing room the night before. Had Irving confided something to him, something he wouldn't tell Stoker or anyone else?

The clothing Collinson had been carrying had looked like the costume Irving wore when playing Mr. Hyde—and the stain on it had looked like dry blood. Hyde committed murder in the play but never appeared covered with blood. What was going on?

Alone in the hall, he looked both ways, then turned the doorknob and entered Henry Irving's dressing room.

Chapter Nine

To the naked eye his hands were clean, yet he could feel the tacky blood between his fingers and smell the bouquet of death beneath his nails. If he closed his eyes and concentrated, he was back in that Whitechapel alley, with the taste of blood on the tip of his tongue. A rush of emotion took his breath away and he shook his head violently to dispel it.

It was afternoon, not at all his time of day. He went out during the day only when it was unavoidable, and when he did he bundled himself up to ward off the sun. When it touched him it was like burning fingertips on his flesh.

He walked to the window and looked out, shielded from the sun by the shadow of the building across the street. The death of the whore in Buck's

Row would sustain him, but he did not know for how long. When the urge returned he would be on the street again, back to Whitechapel, because that was where *they* were. That was his proven hunting ground; that was where they would be waiting for him, calling out to him.

He put his hands on the windowsill, accidentally resting several fingers in a thin shaft of sunlight. He hissed and pulled his hand back, cradled it against his body.

It was getting worse.

Much worse.

Chapter Ten

As promised, Stoker was in his office when Harker returned. He had done a quick search of Henry Irving's dressing room, but since he hadn't known what he was looking for, he didn't find anything. It didn't seem likely Irving would be returning anytime soon, as his dog was nowhere in sight.

Harker sat and read from notes he had taken regarding the three murders.

"Emma Smith was attacked and robbed on Brick Lane, opposite number ten. She went home, and some hours later went to the hospital, where she died as a result of the attack."

"How was she injured?"

"Um, something was, uh, pushed—or inserted—"

"What about your notes, Joseph?" Stoker asked the stammering man. "Just read it from your notes."

"The newspaper said a 'blunt instrument' has been thrust into the woman, and she later expired of 'peritonitis.' "

"How old was she?"

"Forty-five, and she was five-foot-ten."

"What was the date?"

"April third."

"And what about the next one?"

"That was . . . August seventh," Harker said, consulting his notes once again. "This one was Martha Tabram. About thirty-six years old. She was discovered in some place called George-yard, in Whitechapel. She had thirty-nine stab wounds, made by different instruments."

"Not all from the same weapon?"

"According to the report I read, an eyewitness said some of the wounds were deeper than others and could not have been made by the same instrument."

"And the third?"

"Mary Ann Nichols. Stabbed and slashed, wounded so badly that her head was almost"—Harker swallowed—"separated from the rest of her. Also her, uh, private regions were badly cut."

"With the same weapon?"

Harker consulted his notes, which he had written in haste, copying information from an archived issue of *The Times*.

"Apparently."

"Were all three prostitutes?"

"They were considered to be, yes," Harker said. "The second woman, Tabram, had been married but had turned to prostitution after she left her husband."

Stoker sat back in his chair and scratched his red beard.

"What are you thinking?" Harker asked.

"Something doesn't sound right. Are the police certain that these murders were committed by the same man?"

"The newspapers seem intent on connecting them," Harker said. "I do believe from what I read that there were different policemen working on these cases, yet Inspector Swanson did say last night that he was investigating them all."

"He and some others, he said," Stoker added.

"Are you thinking that they have not been committed by the same man?"

"Well—and this is just from your notes, mind you—the first woman was not killed on the street. She went home and later died in the hospital. The second and third women were stabbed, or slashed, and left to die on the street. It seems to me that victims two and three might have been killed by the same man, but not victim one. After all, she was also robbed. Were the other two?"

"Not according to what I read."

"Interesting."

"But what about Conan Doyle's belief that the police already know who the culprit is?"

Robert J. Randisi

"If they do, why would they be forcing us to close down *Jekyll and Hyde*?"

"That's a good point. So the creator of the great Sherlock Holmes might be wrong?"

"Have you read *A Study in Scarlet*?"

"Yes, I have," Harker admitted. "And I greatly enjoyed it."

"Well, as Conan Doyle pointed out to me," Stoker explained, "he's a writer and a physician, not a detective, no matter what he writes about. So yes, the creator of Sherlock Holmes may very well be wrong, in this instance—but let's not try telling him that just yet, hmm?"

"Of course."

"Good."

"What shall we do now?"

"It's getting late," Stoker said. "Why don't you get on home? Will I be able to read your notes if you leave them with me?"

"They're rather hastily scribbled, but I think you can make them out."

"Excellent," Stoker said. "Perhaps something else will occur to me."

Harker rose, approached the desk and handed Stoker his notes.

"What will we be doing tomorrow?"

"We'll go and have a look at the scenes of the crime, I think," Stoker said. "We'll work backward, and go to the most recent one first."

"What about the first woman, Emma Smith? Will we be going to where she was attacked?"

"I'm not sure," Stoker said. "I may decide to treat her murder as something separate. I'll have to think it over tonight. Go on home, Joseph, and thank you. So far you've been invaluable."

Harker straightened. "Thank you, Bram, for giving me the opportunity to help the Lyceum."

With that they bade each other good night and Harker took his leave, with the promise to return early the next morning.

Stoker took the time to go through the younger man's note, which had, indeed, been hastily scrawled. He could barely make out the scratchings, but what stood out clearly were the dates. One in April, and then two in August. This also led him to believe that the first killing—the robbery—did not fit with the other two.

Florence was much better at deciphering the handwriting of others than he. However, he still hadn't decided what he was going to tell his wife. If he admitted to trying to find the Whitechapel murderer, she would probably be convinced he was as mad as everyone else connected with the killings.

He stowed the notes away in his jacket pocket and left the office to go and check on the theater before he locked it up. Once or twice in the early days he had locked some people inside. Since that time he had been very careful about searching the entire building before going home. And after the addition of some electric lights he had to make sure that they were all turned off as well.

*   *   *

He was walking down the hall toward Irving's dressing room, having already inspected the rest of the building, when he noticed a light beneath the door. He had not seen Irving all day, and assumed the man had not returned after leaving with Ellen Terry. Perhaps Collinson had left the lamp in Irving's dressing room lit. The last thing they needed was a fire, so he walked to the door, knocked and entered.

Henry Irving was there, seated at his dressing table, staring into the mirror. The thing that surprised Stoker most was seeing Irving wearing the clothes and makeup of Mr. Hyde. Irving had installed electric lights around his mirror, and they cast a garish yellow light on Hyde's face.

"Uh . . . Henry?"

At first it was as if the man had not heard him, Then, slowly, Irving turned and looked at Stoker with Mr. Hyde's eyes. Stoker immediately became concerned. He had seen Irving immerse himself in a role before, but the look in his eyes was frightening.

Stoker had always found the character of Hyde— the dark side of Jekyll's soul—fascinating. It was that fascination with darkness that had started him on his path toward the book he was preparing to write. Perhaps that was also the reason he was now interested in the Whitechapel killer. If ever a man had gone over to the "dark side," it was that madman.

But here, in this room, in close proximity not to

Henry Irving but to Mr. Hyde, he was torn between fascination and fear.

"Henry . . ."

Irving continued to stare at Stoker as if they had never met—then, with a shake of his head, the character seemed to fade and the actor returned.

"Did I give you a start?" he asked slowly.

"Well . . . yes, actually. Why are you dressed that way?"

"Oh . . . perhaps one last farewell to poor Mr. Hyde."

"Poor Hyde?" Stoker asked. "I would have said 'poor Jekyll.' "

"Ah, but it is Hyde who is lost, is it not, Bram?" Irving asked. "He's the lost soul of Jekyll, and therefore deserving of our pity."

"But he is a killer," Stoker said. "Would you say that this Whitechapel chap is also deserving of our pity?"

"No," Irving said emphatically, "not when he's the cause of my play being closed."

He turned to the mirror and stared at himself again.

"Was there something you wanted?" he asked Stoker.

"I was . . . closing up, chief. I saw the light and—"

"You can go on home, Bram," Irving said, cutting him off. "I will lock up when I leave. I . . . have to remove my makeup for the last time."

"All right, then . . . good night."

"Good night. I'll see you tomorrow."

"There's really no need for you to come in, Henry," Stoker said. "I have some errands to run and will probably be in and out all day, but we do have things in motion for *Macbeth*—"

"I'll come in anyway," Henry Irving said, cutting him short yet again. "I have some . . . things to do myself."

"Very well," Stoker said. "As you wish, Henry."

Irving didn't answer. Once again he seemed lost in the image of Mr. Hyde.

As he left the theater Stoker found himself wondering if that mad devil had actually been in the theater one night, watching the play and Irving's inspired—frightening—performance as Hyde. *Dr. Jekyll and Mr. Hyde* certainly did not start the man killing, but could the police have been right about it urging him on?

Chapter Eleven

September 3, 1888

By the time he arrived home Stoker had decided to confide everything in Florence. He knew she'd be unhappy with the course of action he was taking. But he had not lied to her in the ten years they had been married, nor had he tried to keep anything from her, and he didn't want to start now. His relationship with Florence was the one constant in his life, especially now that he wasn't sure what was happening with Henry Irving.

He entered the house and realized Florence had gone to bed. That was just as well. They could talk in the morning. He still had a lot of thinking to do.

He prepared a cup of tea for himself, grabbed a

biscuit and sat at the kitchen table with Harker's
notes. He tried in vain to decipher them, then decided to simply work with what he remembered.
More and more he believed the first murder was not
connected with the second and third. That would
save some time—if it was true. He was not a policeman, not a detective, but he had personal reasons for wanting to find this killer.

Aside from the fact that he wanted to keep *Dr.
Jekyll and Mr. Hyde* going at the Lyceum, for both
artistic and financial reasons, he wanted to meet the
Whitechapel killer. Not necessarily catch him, but
if he could identify him and give the information to
the police, maybe they would let him see the man,
talk to him. Suddenly this was very important. To
study the dark side of humanity, he had to experience it.

On the other hand, Irving seemed much too taken
with the part of Mr. Hyde. Perhaps having the production closed down would be the best thing for
everyone. Perhaps Stoker should just mind his own
business, prepare for a showing of *Macbeth* and let
the police do their job.

But if they were doing their job, shouldn't they
have caught this madman by now? What if Stoker
identified him and, as a result, women all over London—or at least in Whitechapel—were safe. It
didn't matter that they were prostitutes, they were
still women—people—who deserved to be able to
walk freely through the streets. What if the killer
decided to raise his sights? What if instead of

whores he started going after decent women? Like Florence? Or Ellen Terry?

At last he had come up with a decent argument for him to continue on his set course. He had to help make London safe for all women, lowborn or high.

When Stoker came downstairs the next morning he discovered Florence sitting at the kitchen table with Harker's notes spread out in front of her.

"Are you able to read that handwriting? Harker's penmanship is most abominable."

She stared at him a moment before answering.

"Enough to realize you're mad, and you've gotten this young man involved in your madness."

"Dearest—" he said, reaching for her hand, but she pulled it away, shrinking from his touch.

"Does all this mean what I think it means?" she asked, indicating the scraps of paper.

"Why don't I make us some tea and we can discuss it?"

"I do not want any tea, thank you." Her exquisite gray-blue eyes were the coldest he had ever seen them, sending a chill through him. "I want to know what all this means."

"I think you have already come to a conclusion that is correct."

"You truly intend to pursue this madman?"

"Not to find the madman, per se, but to uncover his identity."

"Semantics." She spoke as if it were a dirty word.

"Florence, my dear, the Lyceum stands to lose a lot of money, which means we stand to lose a lot as well. We need *Jekyll and Hyde* to start up again, and the only way that is going to happen is for this killer to be found."

"By the police!" Florence implored. "My God, you've never been a stupid man, Bram. Why start now?"

The words stung. She had never spoken to him in such a manner. In fact, he could scarcely recall a harsh word passing between them during their entire marriage.

"Florence, you must understand—"

"I can't understand," she said, "and I won't."

"What does that mean?"

She stood up to her full height. She was five-foot-eight, but slight, still dwarfed by his physical size, yet intimidated not in the least. Such was the power of her anger—or fear.

"If you pursue this . . . this mad course of action, I shall not be here when you return home."

"Surely, you don't mean—"

"I do mean it, Bram," she said. "I will pack and . . . and go to stay with my mother."

For a moment he'd been afraid she was threatening to leave him for good. But to have her go to her mother's—perhaps that would be best, after all.

"I warn you," she went on, "I shan't return until you've given up this . . . this quest of yours."

"Florence," he said, lamely, "I have committed myself—"

"Perhaps you *should* be committed," she snapped.

"That's enough!" He barked the words with such force that she stood there, startled. "I'll not have you speaking to me that way. I'm your husband. I think perhaps it is a good idea for you to go to your mother's for a while, Florence. It will free me to do what I must without having to worry about you."

She stared at him, her eyes moist, her expression so fragile, so on the edge, that he longed to reach out and take her in his arms—but he resisted.

"Very well, then . . ." she said. He expected more, but suddenly she straightened her shoulders and walked past him, out of the room. Alone in the kitchen, he gathered the notes from the table and decided to leave immediately. He would get something to eat in London, when he left the ferry.

Chapter Twelve

"I've never been to Whitechapel before," Joseph Harker said.

"Nor have I," Stoker admitted.

The two men looked at each other, then at their surroundings. Both were severely out of their element. They had disembarked from the London Rail at Whitechapel Road and were looking helplessly about.

"I suppose we had better start looking for Buck's Row," Stoker said.

They were intending to work backward, beginning with the site of Mary Ann Nichols's murder.

"Which direction?" Harker asked.

"This way, I think." Stoker had no idea, but they had to start somewhere, so he chose east.

They walked for a few blocks, then headed north and before long came to Wellington Street.

"Can this be the same street the Lyceum's on?" Harker asked. "I didn't know it extended this far."

"Perhaps," Stoker said, "it's time to ask directions of someone."

When they finally found Buck's Row—not far from where they'd discovered Wellington Street—they advanced cautiously, looking for the place where "Polly" Nichols had been murdered. They'd learned she went by the name Polly from the man they'd asked directions of.

"Lookin' for where ol' Polly bought it, are you?" the fellow had asked.

"Polly?" Harker asked.

" 'At's what we all knew 'er as. Mary Ann may 'ave been 'er name, but we all called 'er Polly."

They entered Buck's Row from Brady Street, Harker referring to the notes Stoker had returned to him, trying to locate the exact spot where she had been killed.

"According to the newspaper account, she was found across from Essex Warf. That would be . . . well, here."

Standing in front of the wharf, they looked around and found that they were alone, despite the early hour.

"Seems the locals are avoiding this area," Stoker said.

"I would too, if I lived around here," Harker said,

and then added, "but thank the Lord I don't. The stench!"

Stoker walked along, past the wharf, past Harker, looking down at the cobblestoned street. How much of Polly Nichols's blood, he wondered, had run between these stones? He stopped, finally, when he found some dark stains on the road. He could hear the sound of children, and when he looked to his left realized that he was standing right next to a school. Were these dark stains blood? Polly's blood? Or something else entirely? Was he standing on the exact spot where the madman had stood, or knelt, over her, hands covered by her blood? The air had probably been thick with the smell of it. Had he lifted his hands to his face, smelled her, perhaps even tasted her?

"Bram!"

Stoker became aware that Harker had called out his name several times.

"Oh, uh, sorry," he said, turning to face the other man. "I was . . . thinking."

"Thinking?" Harker asked. "You looked as if you had gone into a trance."

Stoker looked back down at the ground.

"I was just . . . attempting to put myself in the killer's place."

"My God, why?"

Stoker looked at the younger man again.

"I'm trying to understand—"

"What is there to understand?" Harker demanded. "He's a madman."

"I'd like to know what drives him," Stoker explained.

Harker shuddered. "Well, I don't. I can think of many things I'd rather do than have a look inside a monster's head."

As frightening as it seemed, Stoker could think of nothing he'd rather do at that moment.

Chapter Thirteen

Harker stood by nervously as Stoker paced Buck's Row. He was watching Stoker in much the same way Stoker had looked at Henry Irving when last he saw him dressed as Mr. Hyde. Just as Stoker had worried that Irving might be too engrossed in the character of Hyde, Harker was wondering if Stoker wasn't becoming too interested in the Whitechapel murderer.

"Bram?"

This time Stoker responded the first time. "Yes?"

Looking up and down the alley nervously, Harker said, "Isn't it time to be going?"

"In a moment, Joseph."

Stoker continued to stalk up and down until suddenly the doors to the school opened and the chil-

Robert J. Randisi

dren began filing out. Two teachers saw both Stoker
and Harker and eyed them suspiciously, ushering
the children quickly away.

"Why are they looking at us so queerly?" Harker
wondered.

Stoker turned to Harker. "Have there been any
descriptions of the killer?"

Harker referred to his notes.

"Not specifically, but Polly Nichols was seen in
the company of a well-dressed man—apparently in
a cloak and top hat—shortly before she was murdered."

Stoker looked down at himself, and then examined Harker's attire. Both of them were not particularly well dressed for an evening at the Lyceum,
but for a stroll down Buck's Row in Whitechapel
they were extremely overdressed.

"They're wary of anyone well dressed," Stoker
said. "Our man is obviously considered by these
people to be a man of means."

"Then why is he coming down here to kill
women?" Harker asked. "Why not do it in a better
neighborhood?"

"I'm sure there are several answers to that question," Stoker said, "but perhaps the simplest one is
. . . the killer is a snob. Come on, Joseph. Time to
move on."

"Do you want to find where Martha Tabram was
killed?"

"Not yet," Stoker said. "Let's find a pub, have a
pint and perhaps ask a few questions. And where

was the doctor from? The one who pronounced her dead?"

"Um . . ." Harker shuffled papers. "Ah, a Dr. Llewellyn of Whitechapel Road."

"That might be right near here," Stoker said. "Excellent. Perhaps we'll move on to Martha Tabram another day, Joseph. Come long, then. I could use a pint just about now."

"As could I," Harker said, and hurriedly followed Stoker out of Buck's Row.

When they reached Whitechapel Road, Stoker suddenly changed his mind.

"Joseph, do you have the doctor's address?"

"Yes. Thank God for *The Times*. They had almost everything we'd need—here it is. Number one-fifty-two."

Stoker checked the number on the house they were standing in front of.

"It's only a few blocks from here," he observed.

"Why don't we go and get that pint first?" Harker suggested hopefully. "It's too hot out here to be walking around without libation."

"Well," Stoker said, "if we go and talk to the doctor first, perhaps he'll be able to suggest a likely pub. In fact, we might even persuade the doctor to join us."

Harker gave in. "Lead the way, then, Bram. I am only the Watson here. You are the Holmes."

* * *

When they reached 152 Whitechapel Road they approached the door, and Stoker knocked. On the wall next to the door was a shingle with the words DR. HENRY LLEWELLYN, SURGEON. After a moment he was about to knock again, but the door suddenly opened.

"Dr. Llewellyn?"

A man in his fifties said, "I'm Henry Llewellyn."

"The doctor?"

"I am a surgeon, yes."

"Doctor," Stoker said, "my name is Bram Stoker, and this is my . . . colleague, Joseph Harker."

"Gentlemen," the doctor said, executing a slight bow, "is one of you ill?"

"No, we're not ill, Doctor. We, uh, would like to talk to you about Mary Ann Nichols."

"Polly Nichols," Llewellyn said. "What about her? Are you policemen?"

"No, we're not policemen," Stoker said, "but we are . . . investigating her death."

"Investigating?" Llewellyn asked. "To what end?"

Stoker started to answer and then stopped.

"Doctor, I'm an author," he said at last, "and the manager of the Lyceum Theater."

"I have been to the Lyceum, Mr. Stoker," Llewellyn said, "and I have read some of your work. So you see, I know who you are."

"Then perhaps you'll accept our invitation to repair to a pub where we may explain ourselves over a pint."

Llewellyn studied them both for a moment, then said, "What an excellent suggestion."

Chapter Fourteen

They waited while the doctor closed his surgery and then followed him to a nearby tavern on the corner of Whitechapel and Baker's Row. The clientele seemed to be made up of tradesmen and vagrants who had begged enough coin to pay for one drink apiece.

"A poor place," Llewellyn said, "but my local."

They moved in among the crowd of late afternoon drinkers and found a table the three of them could fit at comfortably.

"I assumed that one of you would be doing the buying," Llewellyn said. "My practice does not make me rich."

Stoker looked at Harker and said, "Joseph."

Harker raised his eyebrows, then realized Stoker

was asking him—or telling him—to go to the bar for the drinks.

"Three pints of their finest," Stoker said as Harker stood up. The other man nodded and walked to the bar.

"The young man?" Llewellyn asked.

"He is a scene painter at the theater."

"And an amateur detective?" Llewellyn asked.

"I'm afraid that title refers to both of us."

"And why have you both turned detective?"

Stoker explained about the theater's production of *Dr. Jekyll and Mr. Hyde* being closed down, and why.

"What a preposterous supposition," the doctor responded.

"We all thought so, as well," Stoker said.

At that moment Harker returned, juggling three pints of ale. Stoker and Llewellyn liberated their glasses from him, and he sat down to join them.

"What have I missed?" he asked.

"I was just explaining to the doctor why we are doing what we're doing."

"I hope you told him it was all your idea," Harker said, looking around himself dubiously. Several of the patrons were peering in their direction, examining their clothes. Harker was wondering if he would be able to leave the place with his jacket intact.

"Don't mind them. They think you're a couple of slumming toffs. I don't know what I can do to help you," Llewellyn said to Stoker after a healthy pull from his pint.

"I just want to ask you some questions," Stoker said, "perhaps find out what you saw, what you surmised—"

"I do not surmise anything," the doctor said. "I am not a detective, amateur or otherwise. I examined the body twice, once at the scene and once at the mortuary."

"Doctor, could I bother you to tell us what you learned from the body upon each examination?"

Dr. Llewellyn thought a moment and then said, "All right. I see no harm in that, but it will cost you another pint."

"Done," Stoker said.

"When I arrived in Buck's Row I found the victim lying on her back with her legs straight out. She was most definitely dead, with extensive damage done to her throat. In truth, her head had nearly been severed."

Harker shuddered, but Stoker was unaware of it. He was enthralled by the doctor's narrative.

"While her wrists and arms were cold, her lower extremities were still very warm. I concluded that she could not have been dead more than half an hour. I also noticed that her abdomen had been . . . well, attacked is the best word . . . but it was dark, and I could do no further examination at the scene."

"What about at the mortuary?"

"Ah, well, there I was able to discover much more. Her jaw was bruised, she had bitten her tongue and five of her teeth were missing. There were two incisions on her throat, making it obvious that the first had been botched and was incomplete. The second, however, did the job. There were no wounds between the throat and the abdomen, but the abdomen had many tears and cuts, some of them simply slash marks, apparently made in anger."

"And the weapon used?"

"A large knife with a fairly sharp blade, I would imagine."

"Let me ask you this, Doctor," Stoker said. "Were any of these incisions made with any degree of . . . of actual medical skill?"

"I told the police the same thing when they asked," Llewellyn said. "I think a man with any degree of medical training would have done a much neater job. But I do believe that much of the damage done to this woman resulted from anger, rather than from any . . . ineptitude on the killer's part."

"Do you know anything of the condition of the other two bodies?" Stoker asked.

"Nothing," the doctor said. "Only what I've read in the newspapers, the same as you."

"And do you have any sense of where the police are in this investigation?"

"Confused," Llewellyn said. "Totally baffled."

"Joseph," Stoker said, "why don't you go and get the doctor his second pint?"

Harker himself was only half finished with his own, but he stood and asked Stoker, "And for you?"

"No, just for the doctor."

Harker began to make his way through the crowd to the bar. Stoker sat back, and for a moment he and the doctor sipped their pints and were each alone with their thoughts.

"What's the real reason for your interest, Mr. Stoker?" Llewellyn finally asked.

"I explained about the theater—" Stoker started, but the other man cut him off.

"Yes, yes, I heard all that," he said, waving his hand, "but there must be something else. Are you planning on writing about this?"

"No," Stoker said, "I wasn't planning that at all."

"Have you some sort of morbid interest in this killer?" the doctor asked.

"Well, yes, perhaps . . . I mean, I'm interested in the darker side of men, in what drives them to . . . do some of the things they do."

"And finding this particular man and having the opportunity to talk to him would satisfy some of that?"

"I suppose it would."

"I see." Llewellyn put down his empty glass on the table and leaned forward. Before speaking he looked around, as if afraid someone might overhear.

"Before your colleague comes back there's something else I want to tell you," he confided in low tones. "Something I didn't tell the police."

"Why tell me?"

"I'm not sure," Llewellyn said. "Perhaps I think

you would be able to make some use of it."

"All right," Stoker said with interest. "I'm listening."

"While I was examining the body at the mortuary I noticed something else about the neck, something very . . . unusual."

"And that was . . . ?"

"I found . . . a different kind of mark on her throat, something that was not made with a blade."

"Was this mark inflicted before or after she was dead?"

"That I cannot say."

"What kind of mark are we talking about?"

Again, the doctor looked around before answering.

"Two small holes, here." He touched his own throat on the left side, where his pulse was. "Larger than pinpricks, with some indentations between them."

"Was this caused by her throat being slashed?"

"No," the doctor said, "I'm saying that these holes were in addition to her other wounds."

"And they were made by a different weapon?"

"I don't believe a weapon was used at all."

"Then what do you think made the marks, Doctor?"

Llewellyn looked around quickly, then leaned even closer to Stoker and said, "I won't repeat this to anyone, Mr. Stoker, but . . . I believe they were made by teeth. I believe the killer bit her on the neck!"

Chapter Fifteen

"But was he serious?" Joseph Harker asked Stoker when told later what Dr. Llewellyn had said about the bite mark.

"He was very serious."

They were returning to the Lyceum by rail, having taken the train from Whitechapel Station. They were seated alone in a compartment.

"So he thinks the killer bit her?"

"Believes," Stoker corrected. "He believes the killer bit Polly Nichols on the neck."

"For what possible purpose?"

"He doesn't know," Stoker said. "Since the attack was, in his opinion, driven by anger, this could simply have been another manifestation of that anger, or . . ."

"Or what?" Harker pressed.

"Well . . . it could have been a morbid desire on the part of the killer to . . . taste the blood of his victim."

"Taste?" Harker asked. "You mean bite her neck and suck her blood out like some . . ." He trailed off, but they were both thinking of the same word, which hung in the air between them—vampire!

Upon arriving back at the Lyceum, Harker went in search of his partners to discuss the sets and scenes for *Macbeth*.

"We should, after all, admit that it may come to that," he said to Stoker as they entered his office.

"Yes, of course. As manager of the theater, I, of all people, should admit that. All right, Joseph. I don't want to keep you from your work."

Harker started for the door, then turned back.

"Bram, about this . . . bite . . ."

"Don't speak of it to anyone, Joseph."

"Oh, I won't," the younger man said. "It's just that . . ."

"Just that what?" Stoker asked, a bit impatiently. "Come on, spit it out."

"Well . . . I'm wondering why the doctor would tell you about this, and not the police."

"That's easy," Stoker said with a shrug. "The police would have called him mad."

"And mightn't he be?"

"Did he seem mad to you?"

"No, but . . . I am no authority on madmen."

"The Whitechapel killer is the madman, Joseph, not Dr. Llewellyn. And if what the doctor says is true, this murderer is even more crazed than the police and tabloids imagine him to be."

After Harker left Stoker seated himself behind his desk, replaying the events of the day in his mind. Early that morning Florence had taken her leave, gone to visit her mother until Stoker, she said, had come to his senses. That was just as well, for now he would not have to share this latest bit of information with her. If she knew that he was entertaining talk of a vampire . . .

But he knew little of vampires, other than the legends. Had they ever really existed? And, if they had, were they not the very personification of the dark side of men? And if this mad killer, this slasher of women, actually thought himself a vampire, wouldn't that make him the darkest being of all?

What, he wondered, would it be like to actually stand in the presence of such a man? To perhaps look upon the face of pure evil?

Part Two
Vlad the Impaler

Chapter Sixteen

September 8, 1888

The urge was great, and the reward promised to be greater for Jack, so he gave in.

Back out into the darkness, driven by the hunger . . .

Annie Chapman had no idea what had befallen her. Once again, as had been the case with Polly Nichols, the pass of the knife across the throat resulted in the woman's head being almost severed from her body.

Jack was satisfied with the cut, though—much more satisfied than last time. As a result she lay at

Robert J. Randisi

his feet in the yard behind 29 Hanbury Street, Whitechapel, awaiting his pleasure.

He leaned over her like a lover, but no lover ever wielded his male organ as Jack did his knife. The cuts tonight were deep—deeper than any Polly Nichols's body had suffered. Jack wanted his hands inside the body this time. Her abdomen unceremoniously ripped open, the heat of her closed around him to the wrist as he reached inside Annie, drew out her intestines and held them lovingly in both hands. He brought them to his face, sniffing first and then deeply inhaling their bouquet. It was very dark in the yard, but his eyes were accustomed to it, preferred it, in fact.

He gently laid the intestines over her right shoulder and went back to work with his knife, humming to himself. Had there been witnesses to this horrendous event, they would not have testified that Jack was humming, for the sound could only be heard inside the killer's head.

Tossing his cloak behind him, he removed her uterus—a useless appendage for a common whore, in any case. This he would take away with him, a souvenir of the evening. He set it aside and went back into her with his hands, rather clumsily cleaving away two thirds of her bladder. Some cuts were crude, vicious, others more lovingly executed, with patience and skill. He chuckled as he recalled the reports of his previous conquests in both *The Times* and *The Star*. Some spoke of him as a madman, slashing and ripping at the women, while others claimed his actions might be those of a skilled man—in fact, a medical man.

He would soon clear those assumptions away. It was almost time for him to begin some reporting of his own. The police, and, yes, the press, needed to hear from him, but not quite yet.

There was still more to do. Much, much more to do.

When he was finished he was loath to withdraw his hands from her. Although it was a warm night, his hands cooled when removed from inside her body. For just a moment, with his hands deep inside her, he knew what bliss a fetus must know when floating inside his mother's cavity. But this was no mother—rather a motherless, childless, friendless whore whose very existence was a blight—nay, an offense—to nature.

He looked around to be sure he was still alone, then leaned over the body of poor Annie Chapman and placed his mouth to her neck—that final, bliss-ful kiss before taking his leave.

Finally he withdrew from her and picked up his prize. As he retreated into the night he could not help but leave blood behind, dripping from the sev-ered uterus as he carried it off.

The other, a week ago, had been hard to abandon. He'd lingered over her until he had no choice but to take his leave. This one, however, was easier, as he would take a part of her with him. This, then, made the leaving easier, and gave him a reward for his night's work.

Chapter Seventeen

September 9, 1888

The accounts in *The Times* and *The Star* and other tabloids not only shocked Bram Stoker but seemed to bring him out of the trance he had been in for more than a week.

Since his conversation with Dr. Llewellyn, he and Harker had not been out again to investigate the murder sites. He had gotten caught up in his duties as manager of the Lyceum, dealing with the aftermath of the cancellation of *Jekyll and Hyde*. Some ticket holders wanted their money back; he was trying to hold them off with promises that the theater would soon be showing something just as memorable. On the other hand, actors had to be found in the event they did end up doing *Macbeth.*

He was also still concerned by both Henry Irving's attitude and his behavior. He'd become more reticent than usual, his need for control and his obsession for detail seeming to have dissipated. He had, in effect—and in Stoker's view—become very "Mr. Hyde" in his behavior. He appeared sullen at times, mean at others, and yet still not prepared to fight for what he had, and what he believed in. Stoker felt as if he was fighting all the Lyceum's battles on his own.

But there was another distraction for Stoker, one that was taking up all his free time. That distraction was known as Vlad the Impaler.

Ever since Dr. Llewellyn had spoken to him about vampires, he'd been doing research at the British Museum, finding out what he could about the creatures. Once his research led him to the fifteenth-century Romanian Vlad the Impaler, he became obsessed with the man also known as Prince Dracula. *Dracula,* a new word to Stoker, meant "Son of the Dragon." Stoker read everything he could lay his hands on about Vlad, who seemed to personify everything evil in a man.

Vlad was a warrior first and then a ruler, but one who controlled with an iron and cruel hand. His chosen method of executing his enemies was to impale them on a stake and leave them to die. He ruled from 1456 to 1462, at first killing only his political enemies; in time killing became a way of life for him, and he began to do it for sport, or to relieve boredom.

What Stoker read in that morning's edition of *The Times* shocked him but did nothing to reduce his interest in Vlad. When he read of the condition of the Whitechapel killer's latest victim he immediately thought of similarities between Vlad and the killer. With Florence away, and desperate to tell someone of his findings, he practically dragged poor Joseph Harker into his office that morning.

"What's going on?" Harker asked. "I've been wondering why you suddenly lost interest in your investigation."

"I haven't lost interest, Joseph," Stoker said, "I've been doing research."

"On what?"

Stoker hesitated a moment, then said, "Vampires."

"Oh, God," Harker said, shaking his head. "I thought we'd forgotten about that."

"Just hear me out," Stoker said. "In researching vampires I came across Vlad the Impaler."

"Who?"

"A fifteenth-century ruler in Romania—or, to be more precise, Wallachia, which was southern Romania."

"What has some fifteenth-century Romanian to do with all this?" the confused Harker asked.

"Just let me give you some history," Stoker said, and went on to describe to Harker the bloody rule of Vlad the Impaler.

"I am still confused, Bram," Harker complained. "You've gone from vampires to some ancient prince who liked to impale people on—"

"Here," Stoker said, interrupting him. He began opening books on his desk, looking for passages he had marked. He turned the pages of *An Extraordinary and Shocking History of a Great Berserker called Prince Dracula,* another entitled *The Historie and Superstitions of Romantic Romania,* and finally *Wilkinson's Account of Wallachia and Moldavia* before he found what he wanted.

"Here; it says that on occasion Vlad was known to dip his bread into the blood of his enemies so he could savor the taste of life. What does that sound like to you?"

"Well," Harker said, "he's not actually drinking it—"

"Did you read *The Times* this morning?"

"Of course. In fact, I wanted to talk to you about—"

"Did you read of the condition of the body?" Stoker demanded.

"Disgusting!"

"The intestines being laid over her shoulder, and her uterus being removed?"

"I said I read it," Harker said, growing pale.

"Now listen to this. One of Vlad's lovers once lied to him and said she was pregnant, trying to trap him into marriage. When he found out she lied he used a knife to slash open her body from her vagina to her chest and then across her breasts, in the shape of a *T*."

Harker frowned and shrugged. "Gruesome, but—"

"You're not getting it," Stoker accused. He looked to the book again. "Here . . . he made it a law that any wife who had sexual relations outside of the holy bonds of matrimony would have her sexual organs removed!" Stoker slammed the tomes shut. "Do you see now?"

"I think so," Harker said. "You think the killer is a four-hundred-year-old prince?"

Stoker sat back in his chair.

"I'm not a madman, Joseph," he said, calmly. "Think about what this could mean."

And so Harker took a moment to think, and then another, and then it was as if the light dawned.

"You don't really think the killer is a vampire," he said finally. "You think he might be *like* this Vlad . . . who was also not a real vampire. He was just crazy."

"Obviously."

"As this killer is crazy."

"Yes."

Secretly, Harker rejoiced that Stoker was still rational enough to reason with.

"So he might actually *think* he's a vampire. But . . . what does this mean? What does it tell us?"

"Admittedly, not much about the killer . . . except, perhaps, that he too is aware of the history of Vlad the Impaler."

"So perhaps he is fashioning himself after this long-dead prince?"

"It's possible."

Harker was suddenly on the same path as Stoker, and excited about it.

"Bram, this is information you should pass on to the police. It could be important."

Stoker put his hand on one of the history books covering his desk and tapped the cover of it with his index finger.

"Possibly . . . but . . ."

"But what?'

"Do you think they would believe me?"

"Why not talk with Inspector Swanson?" Harker recommended. "He at least knows who you are."

"Yes, yes," Stoker said, "perhaps I should. . . . Well, thank you for listening to me, Joseph. I needed to say all of this aloud to someone."

"Is Florence still visiting her mother?"

"Yes, she is." While he had told Harker and Irving and a few others that Florence was at her mother's, he had not told anyone the real reason she had gone. "She's extended her stay a few days."

"Well," Harker said, standing, "thank you for confiding in me. Does all of this mean we are going to continue our investigation?"

"Most certainly," Stoker said. "We'll go out again tomorrow."

"What about the remainder of today?"

"I have to think," Stoker said. "Perhaps, as you

said, I should go and see Inspector Swanson with my theory."

As he left Harker seemed pleased that Stoker was considering taking his advice.

Stoker, on the other hand, was wondering if he should, indeed, talk to the inspector, or perhaps have another conversation with Dr. Llewellyn first.

Chapter Eighteen

"Why does this not surprise me?" Henry Llewellyn said when he opened his front door to find Bram Stoker standing there.

"I wanted to talk with you a little more, Doctor," Stoker said. "Are you available?"

"Are you buying?"

"Yes," Stoker said, "I am—as many pints as you can drink."

"Let's go, then." Llewellyn stepped outside and pulled the door shut behind him.

"Don't you have to close your surgery?"

"Mr. Stoker," Llewellyn said, "in case you haven't noticed, my surgery is always closed. Shall we go? Same place?"

*　　*　　*

Stoker hadn't noticed it before, but the pub was called the Bloody Bucket. Very fitting.

It was earlier than last time, and tables were fairly easy to come by. There was no crowd for Stoker to fight on his way to the bar and back with two pints.

"Ahh," Llewellyn said, his eyes lighting up as he lifted the glass to his mouth. He made the same sound again after a few swallows, but with more gusto. "Right, then. How can I help you?"

"I've been doing more research since the last time we spoke. You know, on . . ." He paused and lowered his tone. ". . . on what you told me that you didn't tell anyone else?"

"I see. Have *you* told anyone else, sir?"

Only Harker, he thought, but he lied. "No, I have not."

"Well, then, perhaps you will enlighten me as to this research of yours."

Stoker explained about how his reading had led him to Vlad the Impaler. When the doctor indicated he was ignorant on the subject, Stoker continued, giving the physician the background on the man he had come to think of as "the Dark Prince."

"This is all very interesting," Llewellyn remarked when Stoker had finished.

Stoker, realizing that the man's glass was now empty, said, "Let me get you another."

The doctor did not argue. Stoker returned and placed a fresh pint in front of him.

"So what you are telling me is that you believe

this Whitechapel fellow may be the same type of man your Vlad the Impaler was?"

"Yes."

"You do not believe in real vampires," Llewellyn said, "but in men who act like, or perhaps merely think they are, vampires."

"Exactly." After a moment of silence Stoker asked, "Haven't you wondered about it?"

"I did . . . then, but not since, until last week, when I told you about the bite."

"And since then?"

Llewellyn grabbed his fresh pint and said apologetically, "Not at all. Sorry."

"Doctor, I need your opinion on this."

"Why?" Llewellyn asked. "Mr. Stoker, did you come here so I could tell you there are no such things as vampires? I can't tell you that, sir."

"But, if there are—"

"That's something for you to decide. I can't ease your mind by giving you a definitive answer. And besides, if I told you that vampires do not exist, that would just be my opinion, wouldn't it?"

"But . . . you're a physician—"

"Well, then, you must know other physicians to ask," Llewellyn said. "Perhaps one of them can definitively rule out vampirism in the case of this Whitechapel killer. Or perhaps you could look at your research and decide for yourself."

"Answer me this, Doctor," Stoker implored. "If, indeed, there were a man who was a vampire, who was killing women, wouldn't you say that he was the darkest of men, with the darkest of souls?"

Llewellyn sat forward. "So you are interested in the darkness in men's souls, Mr. Stoker?"

"I am."

"Then perhaps you should realize that if there were such things as vampires, they are undead, and as such have no souls, dark or otherwise."

Llewellyn drained his second pint and set down the glass. "Mr. Stoker, I would appreciate it if you would not come to my surgery to talk about this any further. It's not something I even want to think about. I am sorry I ever responded when the call came for me to examine that poor woman."

The doctor rose and left, but before he did Stoker thought he saw something in the man's face. He thought he saw fear. Closing his eyes, and mind, to what he saw—passing it on to Stoker when he had the chance—was perhaps his way of pretending the problem did not exist—or, at the very least, that it was not his.

Stoker sat back in his chair and thought about the doctor's advice. Find another physician, the man had said. Well, he knew one, certainly, but what would that man think of his questions? Did he want to chance having a friend think him mad?

Chapter Nineteen

When Stoker appeared at Conan Doyle's door in Montague Place his friend invited him to come inside.

"Why don't we go to a pub?" Stoker asked. "I have, uh, something to talk to you about."

Conan Doyle turned his head to look behind him, to see if his wife was near.

"Does this have something to do with what we talked about last week?"

"Yes," Stoker said, "very much so."

"Right, then," Conan Doyle said. "Let me tell Louise I'm going out."

Stoker waited on the doorstep until Conan Doyle returned, and then the two repaired to a pub he and his literary circle of friends frequented. In fact, as they walked to a rear table after collecting their pints from the bar, they encountered Anthony Hope, with whom Conan Doyle was a member of the Authors' Club; and also the editor of the *Daily News,* Sir John Robinson, from the Reform Club. Stoker belonged to neither group. After introductions were exchanged, Stoker rushed Conan Doyle off to speak to him in private.

"You should join our clubs, Bram," Conan Doyle said as the two men sat.

"Perhaps," Stoker said impatiently. "We can discuss that another time."

The physician sat back and regarded his friend critically. "Yes, I can see you have something else weighing heavily on your mind at the moment. Right, then, out with it."

Suddenly Stoker was at a loss for words. How should he approach this? Conan Doyle waited patiently for his friend to form his thoughts.

"How much do you know about vampires?" he finally asked.

Conan Doyle looked surprised but answered the question. "Not very much. In legend they are purported to drink the blood of human beings in order to remain 'alive'—if that is the proper word. Why do you ask?"

"I have come across some information that . . . well, if I told the police they would probably brand me mad."

"I'm intrigued," Conan Doyle said. "Go on."

Stoker told Conan Doyle of the findings of Dr.

Llewellyn, and his subsequent research into vampirism.

"Let me get this part straight in my mind, first," Conan Doyle said, when Stoker paused. "You don't really believe in vampires, right?"

"No . . . of course not."

"So this conversation is . . . hypothetical."

"I would not go that far either," Stoker admitted.

The other man sat back and regarded his friend again.

"All right, then. I suppose I'll simply have to let you ask your questions, and answer them as best I can."

Stoker felt frustrated. Could he go through this without his own friend thinking him mad?

"I suppose what I want to know from you, as a physician, is whether you have ever come across a case of a man . . . drinking the blood of others."

The creator of Sherlock Holmes considered the question for a few moments before answering.

"I certainly know the story of Vlad the Impaler," he said. "I mean, I am not as well versed in it as you obviously are, but I know of him. Have I ever personally encountered this sort of man? No, I have not, and I can safely say I am glad of it."

"Do you believe such men exist?"

"I believe men exist who have fallen prey to all sorts of . . . depravity," Conan Doyle said carefully. "Sexual, certainly, and murderous, obviously. But for a man to actually drink the blood of his victims—"

"Perhaps he merely . . . tastes it?"

"Tastes it?" Conan Doyle said with disgust. He looked down at his pint, which he had not yet touched and pushed it away from him. "I would differentiate very little between drinking and tasting, Bram. Whichever he is doing, he is depraved . . . perverse. . . . I wish I had the vocabulary to describe it. It's . . . sinful . . . sick . . ."

"I agree," Stoker said, "oh, I wholeheartedly agree."

"And in light of what you have discovered, and what you . . . contend, or suspect . . . do you intend to continue your . . . your pursuit of this man?"

Stoker's pint also sat untouched. He dropped his hands into his lap.

"I feel I must."

"But . . . why, Bram? Go to the police with what you know, from your Dr. Llewellyn—"

"He will not repeat this to the police," Stoker said, interrupting him. "He thinks they will believe he is mad. If I go to them without substantiation, they will think me the same."

"Then drop it, my friend," Conan Doyle said. "Drop it."

"I—I cannot."

"Then I ask again . . . why?"

Stoker looked at his friend, unsure as to whether he could put this into words.

"You're an author, Doyle, and a passionate man. I am on the verge of beginning a book that will study the darker side of man. Who better personifies that than this killer?"

"So you feel you will not be able to do this book justice without talking to the killer?"

"Seeing, talking to . . . I don't know. I only know that I have this opportunity. I do not know if I can afford to allow it to pass me by."

"Then talk to your Inspector Swanson," Conan Doyle suggested. "Ask him to let you see the man when he is caught."

"And what if they never catch him?"

"Are you so arrogant as to think you can do a better job than the police?"

"I don't have to catch him," Stoker pointed out. "I just want to find him."

"Now you are dealing in semantics, my friend."

"You sound like Florence."

"And what does your wife think of all this?"

"She opposes it," Stoker said. "She has left me."

"What?"

"Gone to her mother's."

"For good?"

"I don't think so . . . I hope not. I think she will return when this is all over."

"Or if you give up this . . ."

"Madness? Was that the word you were going to use?"

"Folly," Conan Doyle said. "I was going to say folly." The physician leaned forward. He spoke low, but with urgency. "Is this worth your marriage?"

Stoker leaned forward and replied in kind.

"Haven't you ever had a project, Doyle . . . a story, a novel . . . that took up your every waking hour? That literally . . . demanded to be written?"

"There are many men in this room who have experienced that, Bram," Conan Doyle replied, "but I daresay none have had books they would risk their lives for."

Chapter Twenty

They left the pub together, but before parting company outside, Doyle asked, "Did you manage to find your Watson?"

Stoker nodded. "Joseph Harker, one of the scene painters from the Lyceum."

"Have you told him all of this?"

"Most of it."

"And he has agreed to go along with you?"

"I'll tell him the rest of it today," Stoker said. "Then I will let him decide for himself."

"I think that's fair, Bram," Doyle said. "The man should know what he is letting himself in for."

"Doyle . . ." Stoker said, "I'm not mad . . . truly."

"Not mad," Doyle said, "but obsessed, no?"

"I could . . . possibly plead guilty to that."

"I wish you luck, my friend." The two men shook hands.

"Can I come to you . . . if I have some more questions . . . or concerns?" Stoker asked.

"Of course," Conan Doyle said, "or simply to fill me in. Call on me anytime, my friend."

Stoker was both bolstered and deflated by his meeting with his friend. Deflated because obviously Conan Doyle, while his curiosity was aroused, did not feel that Stoker was doing the right—or the prudent—thing. Bolstered because his friend was still willing to talk to him, to hear of his progress.

Stoker used the Burleigh Street door to enter the Lyceum. This meant he would pass Henry Irving's dressing room. As he came within sight of it the door opened and the dresser, Walter Collinson, came out carrying a bundle of clothing. He looked both ways, as if to be sure he wasn't being watched, and then pulled the door closed behind him. Stoker stood in the shadows as Collinson turned and walked right past him to the Burleigh Street door. It was dark in the hall, but Stoker still thought he saw rust or red stains on a white shirt as the older man went by. The clothing seemed to be part of Henry Irving's Mr. Hyde wardrobe.

Once Collinson was gone Stoker came out of hiding, feeling a variety of emotions. He felt silly, suspicious and guilty. He walked over to Irving's dressing room and stopped at the door. He'd found nothing the last time he'd seen Collinson with a bundle of clothing. What made him think he would find anything this time? And what did he expect to find?

The point became a moot one when he tried the door and found it locked. He looked around quickly to see if anyone was watching, then turned and went to his own office.

Stoker remained in his office until late, wanting to catch up on paperwork so that he and Harker could continue their investigation in the morning. He still wasn't sure what he was going to do, however. They could investigate another murder site, either that of Martha Tabram, the woman who had been killed before Polly Nichols, or the fresher site where Annie Chapman had been killed just yesterday. Or they could go and talk to Inspector Swanson regarding his theories.

He was also still wondering about Henry Irving, Walter Collinson and the two bundles of Irving's Mr. Hyde wardrobe that appeared to have been stained with blood.

As he was preparing to leave, the door to his office opened, arresting his motion to extinguish the electric lamp on his desk. Stoker looked up, expecting to see Harker, and was surprised to see Henry Irving enter the room.

"Kind of late for you, isn't it, chief?" he asked the tall, gaunt actor.

"I saw your light," Irving said, closing the door behind him. He was dressed in his usual attire before he went into wardrobe: dark trousers and a white shirt, open at the collar.

"I didn't even know you were in the building."

"I was . . . in my dressing room."

"Ah." Stoker could not call him a liar. When he'd found the dressing room door locked he had not bothered to knock. Irving could very well have been inside.

"Well, I was just getting ready to leave."

"Florence must be waiting for you."

"No" Stoker said, "she is still at her mother's."

"Oh, yes, I forgot." Irving paced. Stoker wondered what was on his mind.

"Was there something you wanted to talk about?"

"Hmm? Oh, no, I just . . . saw the light."

"What are you doing here so late?" Stoker asked.

"Just . . . going over some wardrobe. Wanted to see what we needed for *Macbeth.*"

"I see."

"What about scenery?"

"Harker and the others are working on it as we speak," Stoker said. He hoped Irving wouldn't ask him how far along they were. He had no idea.

"Excellent."

"What about Miss Terry?"

"Ellen is preparing herself to play Lady Macbeth," Irving said. "She will be ready."

"Chief . . . it'll be months before we're ready to actually perform it," Stoker pointed out. "I've still got ticket holders asking for refunds. I don't suppose we could—"

"You will handle it, Bram," Irving said absently. "You always handle things. I have complete faith in you."

Stoker was not even sure Irving knew what he was saying. "Henry," he said, as gently as he could, "is there . . . something else on your mind? You seem distracted."

"Distracted?" Irving asked. "Oh, yes, well, I've been trying to get *Jekyll and Hyde* out of my head and *Macbeth* into it. It's very difficult to have to change shows in midstream."

"I can imagine. So you're having trouble, um, doing away with Mr. Hyde?"

"Hmm? Oh, not just Mr. Hyde." Irving tapped his temple. "There's a lot of Henry Jekyll in there too, you know."

"I see." Briefly, Stoker considered asking Irving about the clothes he had seen Collinson carrying on two occasions, but he could not bring himself to do it. He couldn't bear the thought of having his idol think he was suspicious of him.

"Perhaps we should go," Stoker said. "Would you like to stop for a drink, or something to eat?"

"Hmm?" Still distracted, Irving looked around himself, then focused briefly on Stoker. "No, I don't think so, Bram. I'm going back to my dressing room to . . . to straighten up and get my coat. You go on home. I'll see you in the morning."

"I may have some errands to run tomorrow,

Henry," Stoker said as Irving moved toward the door. "I will probably stop in early and then be out most of the day."

"That's fine," Irving said, opening the door. "Do what you have to do."

Irving turned, then arrested the move and turned back.

"Telephone."

"What?"

"The telephone."

"Graham Bell's telephone? What about it?"

"Remind me," Irving said. "I've been thinking lately we need to get one installed."

"All right," Stoker said, wondering what that had to do with anything. "I'll look into it as soon as I can."

"Good, good . . ."

As Irving left Stoker sat down behind his desk. Should he have asked Irving about the clothing, gotten it out into the open? He tried to think back to the first time he'd seen Collinson with stained clothing. Had it been the day after Polly Nichols was killed? And now he'd seen him today, the day after Annie Chapman's death.

What did that, along with Irving's odd moods of late, have to do with . . . anything?

Chapter Twenty-one

Despite his obsession—or because of it—Stoker had convinced himself that what he was doing was for the good of all.

He returned home that evening and felt a curious emptiness. He missed Florence, but did he miss her enough to give up his quest for the Whitechapel killer? Perhaps, if it were only his quest, he would give it up, but there were others to be considered. Many others, most of them women—not to mention Henry Irving, the Lyceum and all the actors.

He prepared a meager dinner for himself and took it with him into his office. He had brought back with him from the theater all of the books he'd been using for research on vampires and Vlad the Impaler.

He leafed through the books for a short time, but then ended up closing them. He felt he had learned all he could about the darkness of men's souls from reading. The rest was going to have to be learned another way—from firsthand experience. Still, he'd take the books back to the theater, leave them in his office instead of here at home—just in case Florence came back.

Henry Irving sprang to mind. Uncomfortably, Stoker pushed away the books and the remnants of his dinner. He went to the kitchen and prepared a cup of tea. It was while drinking the tea that he mulled things over.

Something was obviously occupying Irving's mind, and it wasn't the telephone. Whatever it was appeared more important to Irving than the everyday operation of the Lyceum Theater, more important than continuing to perform *Dr. Jekyll and Mr. Hyde* and more important than . . . what? Everything else? He was distracted, which was something he never was. The man had the keenest sense of concentration Stoker had ever encountered. What, then, was changing that?

He thought about Inspector Swanson asking about Irving and his Mr. Hyde persona.

Bram Stoker could not imagine that Henry Irving could be the Whitechapel killer. Were the police really considering such a thing? Whatever was bothering Irving, mutilating and murdering women could not possibly be a part of it.

Maybe the thing to do was to go to Swanson and

ask him straight out. Did they suspect Irving? Did they have any evidence? Of course, he wouldn't say anything to the man about the clothing or his own suspicions.

Suddenly he spoke aloud. "Good God! I do have suspicions. I actually think that Henry Irving might be doing something . . . illegal."

He went to bed that night with a tremendous feeling of guilt. Hearing from Swanson might alleviate some of it, but *needing* to go to the policeman at all carried its own degree of guilt.

Chapter Twenty-two

It had only been two days since Annie Chapman's murder and there they were—Stoker and Harker—standing in the yard where she had been slaughtered.

They were in Whitechapel again, and Harker was feeling very uncomfortable. The source of his discomfort was the cheap suit he was wearing. Stoker had suggested they dress down to be less conspicuous.

"I don't understand," Harker said as Stoker studied the ground around them. "What do you expect to find here?"

"Think of it," Stoker said. "A couple of nights ago a woman lay here with her entrails placed over her shoulder."

Robert J. Randisi

Harker shuddered. "I don't want to even imagine it."

Stoker looked at him. "Joseph, what did you think it would mean for us to investigate?"

"I wasn't sure," Harker said truthfully. "I'm still not."

"Well, I wasn't either until I spoke with Conan Doyle," Stoker explained. "He said to look at everything, and to talk to as many people as possible."

"That would defeat the purpose of dressing this way," Harker said, sticking his finger inside his collar, where it was chafing his neck. "We dress inconspicuously but walk around asking questions."

"At least we won't be stared at for the way we're dressed."

"Not until we get back uptown, anyway," Harker groused.

"All right," Stoker said. "I think I've seen all I'm going to here."

The drops of blood leading away from where the body was found stopped at the back of the yard. Apparently the killer had realized he was leaving a trail and had taken steps to stop it.

"Too bad," Harker said. "The police could have followed it right to his door."

"That would have been too easy."

They left the yard and found themselves back on Hanbury Street.

"Where do we go now?"

"Pub crawling, I'm afraid," Stoker said. "Let's walk along until we come to one."

As they walked Harker asked, "Do you truly expect to find this man?"

"Perhaps not," Stoker said. He did not want Harker to know the true extent of his obsession. While he had told Conan Doyle he would give the other man all the pertinent information, he had since changed his opinion of what was and was not pertinent. "Perhaps I simply want to do something to get us back to performing *Jekyll and Hyde.*"

"Then wouldn't talking with the police be the way?"

"I intend to speak with Inspector Swanson on the matter, Joseph," Stoker said. "First, however, I would like to spend the afternoon here. If you would like to go back to the theater, please feel free—"

"No, no," Harker said, interrupting him. "I agreed to help you and I will honor my word."

"All right, then," Stoker said. "The first round will be on me."

They did, indeed, spend most of that afternoon— and several more over the next couple of weeks— going from pub to pub, asking questions about Annie Chapman and the other women, getting very little in reply until Stoker had an idea.

"A reward," he told Harker on the morning of September 22.

"For what?"

"For information about the murders."

"Don't you think that would be dangerous?"

"Has there been a part of going down to White-chapel and asking questions that has not been dangerous, Joseph?"

"Well, no, but this seems like we would be asking for trouble. How much of a reward?"

Sitting behind his desk, Stoker stroked his red beard while considering the question. He'd been neglecting his beard, and it was starting to look a bit wild.

"Not so little that it wouldn't interest anyone," he said thoughtfully, "but not so much that it would tempt anyone to try to steal it."

"Fifty pounds?"

Stoker considered Harker's suggestion. To the people who lived in Whitechapel and frequented the pubs there, would fifty pounds be enough to get someone to talk about the Whitechapel killer?

Probably not . . .

"A hundred pounds, I think," Stoker countered.

"And who do you suppose is going to pay this hundred pounds?" Harker asked.

"The Lyceum will," Stoker said. "I can justify it as a legitimate expense."

"When will we do this?"

"Tomorrow," Stoker said. "There was one particular pub where I had the distinct feeling someone knew something but wasn't talking."

"The Bloody Bucket?"

"You felt it too?"

"I felt we were being watched," Harker said.

"Yes," Stoker said, "but it was more than being watched. Someone wanted to talk."

"How could you have felt something like that?"

"I don't know," Stoker said. "Maybe I'm developing an instinct." Conan Doyle had told him to be open, to use all his senses, to *feel*. Maybe it was finally beginning to happen.

"Like Sherlock Holmes?"

"I hardly think so," Stoker said. "In any case, we shall go to the Bloody Bucket tomorrow and make our announcement of a reward."

"But . . . we won't actually have the money with us . . . will we?" Harker asked worriedly.

"Joseph," Stoker said, "we have not been robbed yet, have we?"

"No," Harker admitted, "but nor have we announced that we have a hundred pounds with us."

Stoker frowned. "You may be right. Perhaps *announced* is not the right word. We'll just let it be known . . . strategically."

Harker was still not sure about this plan, but he remained determined to do what he could to help Stoker in his quest to save the Lyceum's season—and his own livelihood.

"We can start tomorrow," Stoker said, then added, "as long as we are still a team?"

"We're still a team," Joseph Harker said, but to himself he added, "for now."

Chapter Twenty-three

The next afternoon Stoker and Harker once again took the train to Whitechapel. Fairly familiar with the area after days of walking around there, they proceeded directly to the Bloody Bucket.

"You know," Stoker said as they approached the place, "we are going to have to start coming down here at night."

"At night?" Harker repeated. He tripped over a broken cobblestone, righted himself and asked, "You mean . . . after dark?"

"That is what night usually brings," Stoker said, "the dark."

"It brings a lot more than the dark," the other man argued. "It brings out a killer."

"Only on certain nights," Stoker said. "And remember, he kills women, not men." Stoker, a big, barrel-chested man, brought himself up to his full height. "Besides, we're both young and strong."

"I am a scene painter," Harker said, "and you are a theater manager, Bram—"

"And a writer."

"—*and* a writer. Neither one of us knows anything about defending himself on the streets—especially these streets."

"Still," Stoker reasoned, "I don't think he would attack two men, do you?"

"Maybe not, but that doesn't mean somebody else wouldn't."

They reached the pub and entered. At that time of the afternoon it was only partially full, but that was fine for their purposes.

"I gave this some thought last night," Stoker said. "I think we should simply talk to the landlord. I'm sure he can put the word out about the reward."

"Whatever you say," Harker agreed. "It's your plan."

Once again they had affected their idea of dressing down, but still remained the two best-dressed men in the place. As they approached the bar every pair of eyes in the place was following them, including the landlord's.

"Gettin' t'be regular, ain'tcha?" he asked, wiping the bar with a dirty rag.

"Oh, you remember us?" Stoker asked.

The man smiled, revealing an equal amount of space and teeth in his mouth. His face was covered with salt-and-pepper stubble, and Stoker figured his age to be somewhere between forty and fifty.

"Ain't hard t' remember a couple a toffs like you." He looked over at Harker, who cringed.

"Oh, we're not toffs," Stoker said, "but we are looking for something."

"A couple a pints?"

"Hmm?" Stoker asked. "Oh, yes, of course . . . yes, two pints of your finest, please."

"Everyone's watching us," Harker said to Stoker, sotto voce.

"Don't worry about it," Stoker said. "They obviously remember us from the last time. I suppose we do tend to stand out."

The landlord returned with their drinks, told them how much they owed and accepted the money.

"Thank you," Stoker said, taking his pint in hand, "but, uh, we still are looking for something."

"And what would that be?" the landlord asked with a knowing wink. "Girls . . . or boys?" He grinned and looked pointedly at Harker when he said *boys.*

"Oh, no . . ." Stoker said. "No, no, no, nothing like that. You see, what we are looking for is anyone who has information about these odd killings that have been going on."

"You gents ain't police," the barkeep said.

"Ah, no, no, we're not," Stoker said.

"Then why wouldya be lookin' fer such a thing?"

"Curiosity."

The man looked at them as if they were crazy.

"We can pay," Stoker said.

"A hundred pounds," Harker said, a little too loudly.

"Shhh," the landlord said harshly, causing Harker to jump. "Don't be sayin' numbers like that out loud. There's them in here would cut yer ear off for a tenner." He beckoned for the two men to lean in closer. "Is this on the level? Ye've got a hundred pounds ta pay for information on this killer?"

"Well," Stoker said, warily, "not with us, but yes, we'll pay that amount—if the information is good. Do you know anything?"

"I might know someone who does," the landlord said. "I'll have to get back to ye."

"When?" Stoker asked.

"Come back here tonight," the landlord said, "after dark. I'll have somethin' for ye then."

"And what should we do until then?" Harker wondered aloud.

The landlord stepped back, spread his arms and said, "Avail yerselves of all the delights my place has to offer."

"Or perhaps," Stoker said, "we'll walk around a bit."

Again, the landlord leaned in. "If I was you, I wouldn't be tellin' nobody else about that reward yer offerin'."

"And why not?" Harker asked.

The man smiled and said, "I'm afraid someone

will cut yer throat, thinkin' ye've got the lolly on ye."

"Kind of you to be concerned," Stoker said. "We'll be back tonight, sir."

"And bring the money wit' ye," the landlord said. "I should have somethin' for ye."

Outside Harker said, "I don't trust him. We've been asking questions for weeks. Now we offer a reward and within five minutes we've got someone claiming it."

"Perhaps when we return," Stoker said, "one of us should be armed."

"Armed?" Harker asked, aghast. "I certainly don't own a pistol. Do you?"

"Actually, no."

"I wouldn't know what to do with one, in any case."

"Nevertheless," Stoker said, "instead of remaining here in Whitechapel unarmed we should return to the theater."

"Just as well," Harker said. "Now that the proprietor of this august establishment knows about the hundred pounds, I would just as well not wander about."

"Come," Stoker said. "We have time to catch the next train."

"It might even make sense," Harker offered, "to have a chat with Inspector Swanson, now that we know we might have some sort of witness."

"You have a point, Joseph," Stoker said, "but tell me, how much of any of this do you think makes sense?"

Chapter Twenty-four

Soon after Stoker and Harker left the Bloody Bucket the proprietor, a man named Ian Gainsley, waved one of his customers over to the bar. A small, disheveled man in his sixties responded, licking his lips as he did. Known as Lonesome Bill, he hung around several of the pubs during the course of the day, hoping someone would buy him a drink. Lonesome Bill had no friends, and depended on his pitiable countenance to get people to feel sorry for him.

"You want Bill, guv?"

"Bill," Gainsley said, "I have a job for you, and if you do it right I'll be in yer debt."

Bill licked his dry lips again. He knew what it

could mean to him to have the proprietor of a pub in his debt.

"What can Bill do for you, guv?" Bill asked anxiously.

"I want you to deliver a message," Gainsley said, "and it must be delivered within the hour. Got that?"

"Bill understands, guv."

"Okay, then," Gainsley said. "Here it is . . ."

A few minutes after Lonesome Bill left the pub, another man—smaller and even more insignificant looking than Bill—got up from a table where he'd been drinking alone.

" 'Ey, Smelly," the proprietor called.

"Eh?"

"Pay fer yer drinks before yer go, mate."

"What, no credit today?" the small man complained. He dug into his raggedy pockets for some coins, and came out with one he hated to part with. Actually, he hated to part with any of them, because they'd all been earned at the risk of his neck. " 'Ere ye go." He dropped it on the bar and left.

Gainsley picked up the copper and examined it. It was one of many the smelly man had been spending over the past few months. He hadn't yet been able to figure out where Smelly had been getting them, but he would. And when he did he'd lay claim to a good number of them for himself. But for now he dropped it into his cashbox and gave it no more thought. He was more concerned with the hundred pounds those two swells were going to give him.

The knock on his door didn't startle him, but visitors were few and far between, so he was concerned. Usually it was his landlord, or one other person.

"Who is it?" he asked, frowning.

"It's me, guv." The only other person who ever knocked on his door.

Since Jack rarely went out during the day he'd decided he needed a good pair of eyes and ears on the street. He'd found a man who would do this for money and not ask questions. A man who would be properly afraid of him. But this one had been working for him now for three months and it was coming close to time to retire him and find a replacement. After all, how long could money keep a man quiet about the things that had been going on in Whitechapel?

He got up from the small writing desk, walked to the door and unlocked it. When he opened it he towered over the man standing there. He looked up and down the hall to be sure no one was watching.

"I'm alone, guv," the man said, "I swear."

"All right, come in."

He allowed the man to enter, then closed the door behind him. He moved to stand between the small man and the desk, where his sample letters were in plain sight. He didn't want the man seeing the name he'd signed at the bottom. He wasn't quite ready to announce his chosen name to the world—certainly not via some Whitechapel slug who would pass it on for the price of a drink.

"What is it?" he asked.

"There's some fellers lookin' fer ye," the man said.

"I know," Jack said. "They're called police."

"Naw, not these. These is offerin' money—a reward for information about ye."

Jack narrowed his eyes and stared at the man.

"Is this the kind of reward someone like you might be thinking of claiming?"

" 'Oy, not me, guv," the man said anxiously. "I makes plenty with what I gets from you."

"How much is this reward supposed to be?"

"A hundred quid."

"Hmm," Jack said. "I wonder who has a hundred pounds to spend looking for me."

"Beats me, guv."

"How did you hear of this?"

"I was in the Bloody Bucket and heard some talk," the man said. "These fellers is supposed ta be comin' back tonight."

"Really? After dark?"

" 'At's what they said."

"After dark," Jack muttered. His time. He dug into his pocket and took out a few coins. He jingled them in his hands. "You know that what I pay you will eventually add up to more than a hundred pounds."

"I knows it, guv." The man was staring at the hand with the coins.

"And a hundred pounds is not enough money to die for, is it, my friend?"

"Not near enough."

"Certainly not when there's more to be made."

Jack held out his hand and dropped the coins into the waiting, grubby hands. They were quickly secreted somewhere within the rags the man used as clothing. The stench coming off the small man was enough to gag a mule, but with what Jack had been doing, and where his nose had been, he had smelled worse—far worse.

"All right, then," Jack said. "The Bloody Bucket it is."

"Ya want I should be there, guv?"

"Nearby, perhaps," Jack said. "Just keep me informed if anything happens before dark."

"Yessir. You can count on me, guv."

"I know I can, Smelly," Jack said. "Off with you now."

After Smelly left, Jack returned to the desk, and the letters. He hadn't got the wording quite right yet, and now he wouldn't be able to concentrate properly. He was going out tonight, to find out who these men were and why they were offering a reward for information about him. Were they journalists, or private inquiry agents? Or just a couple of nosy gents with nothing better to do?

Whatever the case, Jack was going to show them that a hundred quid could buy them more than they ever dreamed.

Join the Leisure Horror Book Club and
GET 2 FREE BOOKS NOW—
An $11.98 value!

Yes! I want to subscribe to the Leisure Horror Book Club.

Please send me my **2 FREE BOOKS**. I have enclosed $2.00 for shipping/handling. Each month I'll receive the two newest Leisure Horror selections to preview for 10 days. If I decide to keep them, I will pay the Special Members Only discounted price of just $4.25 each, a total of $8.50, plus $2.00 shipping/handling. This is a **SAVINGS OF AT LEAST $3.48** off the bookstore price. There is no minimum number of books I must buy and I may cancel the program at any time. In any case, the **2 FREE BOOKS** are mine to keep.

— Not available in Canada. —

NAME: _____

ADDRESS: _____

CITY: _____ **STATE:** _____

COUNTRY: _____ **ZIP:** _____

TELEPHONE: _____

E-MAIL: _____

SIGNATURE: _____

If under 18, Parent or Guardian must sign. Terms, prices, and conditions subject to change. Subscription subject to acceptance. Dorchester Publishing reserves the right to reject any order or cancel any subscription.

The Best in Horror!
Get Two Books Totally FREE!

An
$11.98
Value!
FREE!

PLEASE RUSH
MY TWO FREE
BOOKS TO ME
RIGHT AWAY!

Enclose this card with $2.00
in an envelope and send to:

Leisure Horror Book Club
20 Academy Street
Norwalk, CT 06850-4032

Chapter Twenty-five

The weight of the pistol felt unnatural in Bram Stoker's pocket, and yet oddly comforting. It had scared Joseph Harker when he showed it to him—but in reality, Harker too felt comforted by its presence.

The walk from the Whitechapel train station to the Bloody Bucket was a tense one, the way only intermittently lit by street lamps. Harker jumped at every shadow. Stoker was only marginally better, as he jumped at every other one.

When they entered the pub this time it was almost bursting at the seams. Stoker and Harker saw a prostitute servicing her customer in a corner of the room. Apparently this was the extent to which the murders had driven people indoors.

"Look at that—" Harker started.

"Never mind," Stoker said, cutting him off.

They shook off the advances of two other prostitutes on their way to the bar, pitiable creatures either too old or too sick to be taken seriously by any of the customers.

At the bar they managed to squeeze into a space large enough for one and catch the attention of the landlord.

"Ah, ya made it, lads," Gainsley said, smiling his gap-toothed smile at them.

"Do you have that information for us?" Stoker asked.

Gainsley looked around, then beckoned the two of them to move to the end of the bar with him. When they got there the landlord made two men move so that the three of them could put their heads together. That close, Stoker and Harker could smell the liquor on the man's breath, and the stench that emanated from his armpits.

"I don't have it for ya, but somebody else does."

"And where is this somebody?" Stoker asked.

"Around the corner."

Stoker and Harker exchanged a glance. Stoker could see that Harker was anxious.

"Which corner, landlord?" Stoker asked.

"You go out the door, make a left, walk two blocks. You will come to an alley. Walk down the alley to the end. He will be there waiting for you."

"Who will?" Harker asked.

"His name is Chester."

"Just Chester?" Stoker asked.

"Just Chester," Gainsley said.

"And he has information about the killer?" Stoker asked.

"He has information about many things, my friend," Gainsley said. He had to raise his voice to be heard by them, and yet he was not heard by anyone else. It was a place where people minded their own business—*most* people.

"And I suppose you expect us to pay you?" Harker asked.

Gainsley looked surprised, scratched his stubble.

"Pay me? What fer? I ain't got the information. Chester's got it. You pay him."

"Oh, I see," Harker said. "And you'll get yours from him."

Gainsley pinned Harker with a hard stare that made the scene painter squirm.

"Hey, friend," the landlord said, "you'll be gettin' yours. Whatayou care where I get mine?"

"We don't," Stoker said, putting his hand on Harker's arm. "When do we meet with Chester?"

"Wait 'til midnight."

"Midnight?" Harker repeated. "That's hours away."

"Stay here and have a few drinks 'til then," Gainsley suggested. "First one is on the house."

"Here?" Harker looked appalled.

The landlord leaned even farther over the bar, to the point where Harker found himself moving away.

"Believe me, lad," he said, "you don't want to go out there and wander aimlessly about."

No, Harker found himself thinking, actually I don't.

Chapter Twenty-six

The hours spent in the Bloody Bucket were educational, to say the least. Possibly even fodder for future writings by Stoker. For Harker, however, they were memories better left forgotten. He heaved a sigh of relief when it was finally time to leave.

Going outside, they followed the landlord's directions to the mouth of the alley.

"There's not much light," Harker said.

"It looks like there's a lamp at the end, though."

"Do you have that gun?" Harker asked.

Stoker took the weapon out of his pocket and showed it to him.

"What kind is it?"

"I don't know," Stoker said. "I'm not particularly educated about guns." He put it back in his pocket.

"But you do know how to shoot it, right?"

"Of course. You point it and . . . pull the trigger."

"Have you ever fired a gun before?"

Stoker shrugged. "How hard could it be?"

Harker was anything but comforted as they started walking down the alley, toward the light. Stoker, a big man who always thought he would be able to defend himself in any situation, was tense.

Suddenly Stoker was very aware that he was a writer, and that Harker was a scene painter. Why had he insisted on dragging the other man to the armpit of London looking for a mad killer?

What would they do if they found him?

"That is far enough," a voice said from the darkness.

Stoker and Harker had almost reached the end of the alley. There was one lamp, and while it illuminated them, the speaker stood in the shadows.

"Are you Chester?" Stoker asked.

"Did you bring the hundred pounds?"

"If you have information for us," Stoker said, "then we have the money."

"If you have the money and turn it over," the disembodied voice said, "then we'll let you live."

"We?"

Suddenly there was movement. They realized they were surrounded and were about to be robbed, perhaps killed.

"Take out the gun," Harker said urgently.

"Don't move!" the voice called out. "We only want the money."

"The gun!" Harker shouted.

Stoker grabbed for it. As he tried to pull the gun free the barrel caught on the cloth of his pocket.

"Get them!" the voice called.

There was a flurry of activity in the alley, much of it in the dark. Harker went down. He had either tripped or been struck, Stoker didn't know which for sure. As Stoker turned to face the men who were charging him, suddenly there was another presence in the darkness. Stoker saw a glint of silver, and a splash of red. Two men were down, as something wet struck Stoker on the hand and sleeve. Obviously, two of the would-be attackers had been injured, and possibly killed. He tried in vain to see who was attacking them but could only make out a darkened figure. The third man tried to scream, but the sound caught in his throat and he fell to the ground with blood flowing from a gash in his neck. Someone with a knife and an uncanny ability with it had handled the three men with ease.

The fourth man, Chester, watched the action with horror. Gainsley had not told him that these men were dangerous or he would have brought more help. By the time he realized that Harker was unconscious and Stoker had not laid a hand on anyone, he was seized in an iron grip, lifted off his feet from behind and pulled into the darkness.

"Who are you?" a voice asked Stoker.

It was a different voice, much deeper and more educated, not Chester—or was this the real Chester? Stoker still could not make out anyone in the shadows. The light shining on him kept his eyes from adjusting.

"I—my name is Bram Stoker."

"The writer?" the voice asked.

"Y-yes, I'm a writer."

"Why are you looking for me?"

"For . . . you?"

"You've been asking questions, offering a reward," the voice said. "These . . . vermin were going to kill you for the money,"

Stoker thought he could hear someone trying to speak, but only a croaking sound came out.

"My friend needs help."

"He is not seriously injured," the voice said. "The same cannot be said for the others. They are all dead . . . and this one soon will be."

"Is that . . . Chester?"

"I don't know his name. It doesn't matter. Why are you here?"

"He was going to sell us information about . . . uh, you."

"Why are you looking for me?" the man asked again.

"I—I wanted to talk to you."

"About what?"

"About . . . the killings. About why you do what you do."

"You are not a policeman?"

"No."

"You are not working with the police?"

"No."

"Why would you do something as foolish as looking for me?" the man asked. "Weren't you afraid I would kill you?"

"Well . . . s-so far you've only killed women. I mean, if you are indeed the . . . the Whitechapel killer."

"I am who I am," the man said.

"I just . . . wanted to . . . to talk with you, find out why you . . . you're doing what you're doing."

"For a tabloid story?"

"I am not that kind of writer." Stoker decided to be honest. Perhaps it would save his life. Perhaps the man didn't plan to kill him at all—not after saving them from those others.

"I am planning to write a book . . . about the dark side of man."

There was no response.

"You must admit," he went on, "what you are doing comes from . . . an evil place."

"Does it? I admit nothing," the man said.

"Why—why did you come here?" Stoker asked.

"I heard you were offering a reward," the voice said. "I have been watching the Bloody Bucket. I followed you here."

"To . . . kill me?"

"Perhaps, but first to find out who you were."

"And now that you know?"

There was a moment's hesitation. "I must admit you intrigue me, Stoker. This book you are planning—it is to be a novel?"

"Yes, but I wish to write it based on real feelings and emotions. I have researched—"

"Perhaps," the man said, from the shadows, "we shall talk about your research some other time."

Stoker was about to speak when the body of a man—Chester?—came flying out of the darkness toward him and landed at his feet. The way it landed, like a sack of meal, made it obvious that he was as dead as his comrades.

"Please," Stoker called out, staring into the darkness, "what's . . . what's your name?"

At first there was no answer, and he thought the man had gone. Then the voice seemed to be coming from . . . above.

"I am not quite ready to name myself yet, writer," it said, "but you may call me . . . Jack."

And then he was gone.

Chapter Twenty-seven

"He said his name was Jack?" Inspector Swanson asked.

"That is what he said," Stoker replied.

"You're sure about that?"

"Very."

Stoker looked past Swanson to see how Harker was holding up. He'd been able to rouse the younger man after Jack left. Happy that his friend was alive, he left him sitting on a crate in the alley with bodies strewn about while he went for help. He managed to find a policeman nearby, told him that some men had been killed and then, after he had convinced the man that he wasn't drunk or hallucinating, he'd told him to call for Inspector Swanson. That done, he'd gone back to wait with Harker, who sat for most of the time holding his head in his hands.

"How is Harker?" Stoker asked Swanson.

"Who?" The inspector turned and saw who Stoker was referring to. "Ah, yes. He took a blow to the head, but he'll be fine. You didn't see him get hit?"

"No," Stoker said. "He was suddenly on the ground. I didn't know if he had been struck, or perhaps tripped. Then I was being attacked . . . only I wasn't."

"Right," Swanson said, "because this fellow Jack, who you say is the Whitechapel killer, rescued you and did away with all the villains. Do I have this straight now?"

"That's what happened, Inspector."

"Look," Swanson said, "I want you to come to the local nick with me and we'll talk there. Shall I have someone see your colleague home?"

"That would be a good idea," Stoker said. "Let me go and tell him."

"Right," Swanson said, putting away the pad and pencil he'd been holding. "Maybe this will make a little more sense over some tea."

Stoker walked over to where Harker was seated, still being tended to by a policeman.

" 'E's had a bit of a 'it on the 'ead, sir," the policeman said, "but 'e'll be fine, 'e will."

"Thank you," Stoker said. "May I speak to him for a moment?"

"As you wish, sir," the policeman said, and backed away.

All around them bodies were being lifted up and carried out of the alley.

"Joseph, how do you feel?"

"Bloody awful," Harker said. "My head feels like it's going to fall off."

"The Inspector is going to have a man see you home," Stoker said. "That is, unless you'd rather go to hospital?"

Harker looked at Stoker. The alley was now being illuminated by several lamps held by policeman—policeman who were looking about, causing shadows to shift and move as well.

"No, no hospital," Harker said. "I just need to get home. But what about you—"

"I'm going to talk to the inspector a bit longer before I leave," Stoker said. He put his hand on Harker's shoulder. "I'm bloody sorry I got you into this, Joseph."

"You didn't exactly twist my arm, Bram," Harker said. "I'll see you in the morning at the theater, then."

"Don't bother to come in if you're not feeling up to it," Stoker said. "We can talk later in the week."

"I'll be in tomorrow," Harker said with certainty. "I want to know what the hell happened here tonight."

Stoker patted Harker's shoulder and said, under his breath, "As do I."

* * *

"What were you bloody thinkin'?" Swanson shouted at Stoker.

Stoker had not expected this explosion. They had gone to the local police station, where Swanson had been given an office to use for their conversation. Both had removed their coats and been brought cups of tea, and then Swanson had walked to the door, closed it and whirled on Stoker, shouting.

"Here, now, you've no right—" Stoker started.

"Don't go getting on your high horse with me, Stoker," Swanson said. "I've got every right to carry on if I like. You could have got yourself and Harker killed tonight."

"We . . . I thought I knew what we were doing," Stoker said meekly.

"You had this?" Swanson said, holding Stoker's revolver in one hand. "Only this with which to defend yourselves? It's a damned prop!"

Stoker had gotten the gun from the prop room of the Lyceum. He knew it wouldn't fire, but it was somehow comforting to have it with them. Harker had not known it was a prop.

"Inspector," Stoker said, "I know what we did might seem foolish—"

"*Might?*"

"—but I did manage to come up with a name, didn't I? For your killer?"

"Oh, yes," Swanson said, setting the prop pistol down on the desk with a bang. He walked around the borrowed desk and sat behind it, ignoring his cup of tea. "Jack, wasn't it?"

"That's right."

"Jack," Swanson said again, stroking his mustache, then tugging at it. "That'll narrow the field now, ay?"

"Now wait a minute—"

"Let me tell you what we have, Mr. Stoker," Swanson said. "We have you and Mr. Harker in an alley with four dead men. You say the men were attempting to rob you, but you were rescued by the Whitechapel killer, who you have been looking for, and who told you to call him Jack."

"That's right."

"You're a big strapping man, Stoker," Swanson said. "How do I know you didn't kill those men?"

"I—I?" Stoker stammered. "Kill four men with my own hands?"

"Why not?" Swanson said. "You're big enough and strong enough, aren't you?"

"Perhaps . . . one . . . but certainly not four. Besides, I told you, those men were flung about like rag dolls. The man had amazing strength—"

"Jack," Swanson said. "We're talking about Jack, again."

"Yes."

"He was in front of you, in the shadows."

"Yes."

"You could hear him but not see him."

"That's correct."

"And then he disappeared, leaving you and Mr. Harker alive."

"Yes."

"But he didn't pass near you?"

"No."

"How did he get out of the alley, then, Mr. Stoker? Did he just fade into the walls?

"I don't know," Stoker said. "There must have been a door—"

"There were no doors in the alley, Mr. Stoker," Swanson said. "Ahead of you was a brick wall, that's all."

"Well, then, he must have gone . . . over."

"The wall is fifteen feet high!" Swanson said. "Are you telling me that your friend Jack jumped or flew like a bird over that wall?"

"Look here," Stoker said, "I've told you the truth."

"Tell me, Mr. Stoker," Swanson said, "why would a man who has killed four women—maimed and mutilated them—leave you and your friend Harker alive."

"I believe he was curious."

"Curious about what?"

"About why we were looking for him. He seemed . . . interested in the fact that I am a writer. I mean . . . he knew who I was, recognized my name."

"How very flattering for you, sir," Swanson said.

"Well . . . yes . . ." Stoker said, lamely.

Swanson sat back in his chair. This time he was chewing on his mustache as he regarded Stoker.

"Can you appreciate how . . . fantastic all this sounds? A cold-blooded killer of women kills four men—four villains, admittedly, since we recognized some of them—to save your life and then . . . vanishes?"

"He did say that we might talk again," Stoker said.

"If he is indeed the Whitechapel killer—and I'm just supposing he is for a moment—how do you feel about him knowing your identity? It wouldn't be difficult for him to find out where you live. Perhaps come and see you? How do you feel about that?"

"If he did pay me a visit," Stoker said, "and you had some men there, you'd have him."

"Ah," Swanson said, "I've got men all over the city looking for this madman and you want me to have some of them just sit and watch your house until he shows up?"

"Do you have a better idea?"

"Well," Swanson said, "I could put you in a jail cell."

"Why would you do that?"

"Oh, perhaps for your own protection . . . or perhaps because it makes more sense that you killed those men yourself—oh, probably in self-defense, but we could let an inquest decide that."

"An inquest!" Stoker sprang to his feet. "Now see here, why should I be the subject of an inquest—"

"Oh, do sit down, Mr. Stoker," Swanson said, waving at the writer, "before I put you in a cell just for being a bloody nuisance. I know you didn't kill those men."

"You do?" Stoker sat down again.

"If you had brawled with four men your hands

169

would surely be bruised and bloody, as would your face. You haven't a bruise on you. Of course, the same can't be said for your Mr. Harker."

"He was struck by one of those villains . . . wasn't he?"

"And knocked unconscious," Swanson said. "Very convenient for you."

"What does that mean?"

"It means that you are the only witness to the arrival of this Jack fellow."

"But he was there!"

"I'm sure someone was there, Mr. Stoker," Swanson said, "someone who helped you and *claimed* to be the killer."

"What do you mean *claimed?* Who would claim such a thing if it were not true?"

"Oh, believe me, sir," Swanson said, "we have had many men—and women—come in here swearing to be the Whitechapel killer. They crave the attention."

"That's . . . mad."

"Sad, is what it is, sir," Swanson said. "For some people it's the only way anyone sees them."

"I can tell you, Inspector, I am quite convinced that the man I spoke to tonight was the killer."

"Indeed. And of course you bring with you years of experience dealing with criminals to make that observation?"

"Well . . . no . . . but . . ."

Swanson took a deep breath and closed his eyes as he let it out slowly. A great, cleansing sigh.

"Mr. Stoker," he said, "I think you should go home and leave the policework to the police."

"But . . . you do believe me, don't you?"

"Let me ask you something, sir."

"Go on."

"Could the man you spoke to have been Henry Irving, dressed as Mr. Hyde?"

"That's preposterous!" Stoker shouted, almost bolting to his feet.

"Isn't Mr. Irving capable of voice changes? I mean, isn't that something actors are proficient at?"

"Whatever voice Henry Irving might affect I would recognize it," Stoker said. "Why would you ask me such a question?"

"Why would you involve yourself in this affair, sir? Unless it was to try to clear the name of your . . . employer?"

"I want the Lyceum to be able to continue with *Dr. Jekyll and Mr. Hyde*. That is all. Why would you suspect Henry Irving of any wrongdoing?"

"You yourself brought his name up in conversation, remember?"

"*You* brought up his name."

"Ah, yes," Swanson said, "it was you who proffered up the prime minister as a suspect."

"That was only an example of how ludicrous it was for you to suggest Irving!" Stoker was becoming exasperated. It was clear that Swanson did not appreciate his help—or interference, depending which side you were on—and did not believe that he had spoken with the actual Whitechapel killer.

If that was, indeed, the case, then he was wasting his breath trying to convince the man.

Stoker stood. "If you have no further questions, Inspector, I think I will leave now."

"No questions," Swanson said, "just some advice. Don't go traipsing around Whitechapel, Mr. Stoker, either in the daytime or at night. You and your theater friends are not cut out for it."

"I understand."

"And, as I said before, leave the policework to the police. If you want to try to have the ban on your show lifted, do it through your own social or political channels."

"My channels—"

"Isn't that what you people do to get what you want?" Swanson went on. "Pull strings?"

Chapter Twenty-eight

The killing of the men was not as satisfying to Jack as the killing of the women. He washed, trying to get the stench of the brutes off him. When he returned from dallying with his "ladies" he usually reveled in the fragrance that clung to him—the scent of their skin, the odor of their warm blood, the taste of their fear.

He dried his hands, face and chest and set the towel aside. Bare-chested, he walked to the window and looked out at the dark streets. What an intriguing turn of events to find Bram Stoker interested in him. Jack was actually quite flattered. Of course his exploits had been written up in the newspapers, but perhaps Stoker wanted to write something more substantial about him. For that to be done, however, he had to step out of the shadows and take on a very definite identity. That meant he was finally going to have to settle on his name, and finish writing his letter. The question was to whom to address the letter. The police? The press? That could come later. The salutation he had in mind would fit into either scenario.

He walked to the writing desk, sat down, pushed aside all the aborted attempts and addressed a clean sheet of paper with quill in hand. After only a moment's deliberation he dipped the tip and proceeded to write, "Dear Boss . . ."

Chapter Twenty-nine

It was several days later that Harker returned to the Lyceum. He had sent word that he was feeling ill, but Stoker had still been on the verge of visiting him.

"It's so good to see you," Stoker said as Harker entered his office. He stood and shook Harker's hand heartily. "How are you feeling?"

"I visited my own doctor, who said he thought I had suffered a concussion," Harker explained. "I was dizzy for a while, but it seems to have cleared up."

"Well, sit down, sit down," Stoker insisted. "Are you sure you're fit to return?'

"Quite fit," Harker said, seating himself, "but I

did want to talk to you about this, uh, Watson business."

Stoker leaned on his desk, listening attentively. There was barely room for him to lean, however, for the desktop was covered by his research books.

"Say whatever you feel you must, Joseph."

"Well . . . I just don't think I'm cut out to be Dr. Watson to your Sherlock Holmes, Bram. I wasn't struck by anyone, you know. I panicked and got tangled in my own feet. I simply . . . tripped and hit my head."

"Say no more, my dear fellow," Stoker said. "I completely understand. To tell you the truth, I'm having my second thoughts about playing Sherlock Holmes myself."

"Really?" Harker looked tremendously relieved. "That's wonderful!"

"Yes," Stoker said. "So you see, you can just concentrate on the scenery for *Macbeth.*"

"I don't mind telling you, I do feel better ridding myself of this affair," Harker said. "I mean, I'm not a coward or anything, but that whole scene in the alley—I still don't know how we got out of there alive."

"We had help."

"Yes, I heard you telling the inspector," Harker said. "You really believe the killer was there?"

"Yes, Joseph," Stoker said, "and he spoke to me."

"So he knows who you are?"

"Yes."

Suddenly Harker looked frightened. "Does he know who I am?"

Stoker stood up and placed his arm around Harker's shoulder, pulling him to his feet as well.

"He has no idea who you are, my friend," he said, leading Harker to the door. "You've no need to worry."

"Good, good," Harker said. He turned to face Stoker. "I'm so glad you've decided to give up your investigation, Bram."

"Yes," Stoker said. "Now we can all get back to what we do the best."

After he had ushered Joseph Harker from his office, Stoker returned to his desk and seated himself. It was necessary to lie to the man so he would not feel badly about his decision to stop playing Dr. Watson. In truth, Stoker had considered giving up his investigation into the Whitechapel killings, but he remained convinced that the man he had spoken to in that alley several nights before was the actual killer. With that kind of contact made, he simply could not give up his quest. At this point his goals— having the ban lifted from the Lyceum's performance of *Dr. Jekyll and Mr. Hyde,* and learning something about the dark side of man from the Whitechapel killer—had melded into one.

He sat back in his chair, reviewing the myriad of emotions he'd gone through over the past few days—fear being primary among them—until finally reaching the point he was at now—

exhilaration. After all, he had managed what the police could not after four murders; he had spoken to *the man himself.* Inspector Swanson and all his resources had not come close to such a discovery. The fact that a layman had done so probably rankled, which accounted for the refusal of the police to believe him. In any case, he now knew the killer's name—Jack.

Of course, by the same token, Jack now knew his identity. That was where the fear factored in. Inspector Swanson was right when he said it wouldn't be hard for the man to find out where Stoker lived. It was also no secret that he managed the Lyceum, the most successful theater in London. Good Lord, what if the killer *had* been to the theater in the past, and *had* seen *Jekyll and Hyde*? Could the police be right about the play inciting his blood lust?

No, that was still a preposterous assumption, a ridiculous premise on which to base any actions. The man in the alley was obviously well spoken and educated. Whatever was driving him to kill, it was not a play, no matter how brilliant Irving's performance was.

The question now was whether Stoker should continue to wander the streets of Whitechapel without Harker, in search of a clue to the killer's identity, or wait for the killer to contact him?

Ultimately, he was excited by the possibility of the killer contacting him, having come to terms with the fear and set it aside. Perhaps the killer actually needed someone to talk to, to confide in, and since he knew Stoker was a writer, perhaps he would choose him. After all, no matter what a man's accomplishments might be—even murder—wouldn't he want to be remembered, perhaps even immortalized? And who better to do that for him than a writer?

Stoker turned in his chair and stared out the window. He thought back to that night in the alley, back to the way the killer had so easily dispatched those four men. How had he disappeared from the alley the way he had?

Chapter Thirty

Stoker was walking through the theater a few nights later, dousing lights and checking to make sure the building was empty before he locked up. He was startled to find someone sitting in the front row, staring up at the stage. As he walked down the aisle he could see it was a woman. Finally he recognized Ellen Terry.

"Ellen?"

She turned, also startled for a moment before recognizing him.

"Oh, Bram. You gave me a fright."

"I'm sorry. Are you all right?"

"Oh, I'm fine."

He walked over and sat next to her. He looked at

her fine, classic profile as she turned her head to stare at the stage again.

"What are you doing here?" he asked.

"I'm not sure," she said without looking at him. "I think I was waiting for you."

"For me? Or Henry?"

This time she looked at him as she answered. "For you, but it's about Henry."

"What about him, Ellen?"

"I'm concerned about his health."

"Why?"

"He doesn't seem very concerned about getting ready for *Macbeth*. It's as if he doesn't want to let go of *Jekyll and Hyde.*"

Or maybe just Mr. Hyde, Stoker thought.

"He's not himself," she went on. "He's . . . distracted, sloppy, moody . . . not Henry at all. Surely you've noticed."

"Yes, Ellen," Stoker said, "I've noticed."

"You're his friend, Bram. You know him best."

"Not best," he said, "but I am his friend."

"Can you explain it, then?"

He had his theories, of course, but none he wanted to voice to her. Instead he took her hands in his and held them, trying to reassure her.

"Don't worry, Ellen. Whatever is bothering Henry I'm going to get to the bottom of it. I promise."

"I don't really care if we do *Jekyll and Hyde* or *Macbeth,*" she said. "I just want Henry to be . . . well, Henry."

He rubbed her hands and said, "I'm working on it, Ellen. Now come; I'll take you outside and put you in a cab to your hotel."

On the street, as a cab slowed in response to a wave from Stoker, Ellen Terry asked, "How is Florence, Bram? I haven't seen her in quite some time."

Florence was still at her mother's, but he didn't want to tell her that.

"Florence is fine, Ellen," he assured her. "She's keeping herself busy these days."

"Tell her I said hello, will you?"

"I will." He helped her into the cab and closed the door. "Get some rest. I'll see you tomorrow."

"Good night, Bram," she said, touching his arm for a moment, "and thank you."

He banged on the door as a signal to the driver to move on. Then he returned to check the backstage area before locking up.

Of late, whenever he approached Henry Irving's dressing room Stoker did so with caution. He had not seen Collinson leave the room with bloody clothes since the day after the last murder. He had still, however, on more than one occasion discovered Henry Irving seemingly in the grip of some sort of malaise. He did not believe Irving was a killer, but he was convinced that there was something wrong with him. What he didn't know was whether it was physical or mental.

When Stoker left the theater he did not want to

go home. Once he was there he missed Florence terribly. He wanted to go to her mother's and fetch her, bring her home, but he knew she would not stay if he continued to pursue his present course, and he wasn't quite ready to give it up. Also, it would not do to have Florence home when the killer could easily discover where they lived. No, she was safer where she was.

He went, instead, to the pub where Conan Doyle and his literary brethren spent much of their time. Sherlock Holmes's creator was not present. As Stoker made his way to the bar he passed one or two of the people to whom Conan Doyle had introduced him, and exchanged simple greetings, just a slight nod of the head to acknowledge each other's presence.

At the bar he ordered a pint and nursed it. He listened to snatches of conversation around him but in the end had to admit that this was doing nothing to help him. His only supports in his actions had been Harker and Conan Doyle, neither of whom was present. In any case, Harker had effectively withdrawn his support this day. In the absence of Conan Doyle—his only remaining confidant— Stoker abandoned the remainder of his pint and left the pub.

Part Three

Yours Truly,
Jack the Ripper

Chapter Thirty-one

September 25, 1888

Stoker had checked the entire theater. It was empty and locked up tightly. Even Irving's dressing room was empty, with no sign of him or Collinson. Since the incident in the Whitechapel alley three nights before it had been business as usual around the theater. Everyone—actors, scene painters, stagehands, even Stoker himself—had been preparing for the opening of *Macbeth*. There had been no women killed since September 8, and no sign of the killer since the night in the alley. Likewise, Stoker had not spoken to Conan Doyle in days. In addition, he was still stinging from the tongue-lashing given him by Inspector Swanson.

As he headed back to his office to retrieve his top coat he was giving serious thought to going to Florence's mother's house the next day and persuading her to come home. The more he pondered it, the more ridiculous the idea of the killer contacting him seemed to become. After all, he was a theater manager and a writer. What possible reason could there be for the killer to do so?

Walking down the hall, he heard what sounded like a door closing behind him—but all the doors had been locked. He stopped and turned to peer into the darkness.

"Hello?" he called. "Anyone there?"

No answer. He started for his office again, but turned quickly when he thought he heard someone behind him. He felt silly when he saw that no one was there. With all this thinking about the killer he had made himself nervous. The smart thing to do would be to go and get Florence and bring her home. She was his rock, she was his—

No, there it was again. Someone was walking; he could hear their footsteps echoing.

"Hello? Who's there? This building is supposed to be locked—"

"Locked to other people, Mr. Stoker," a deep voice said from the shadows, "but not to me."

The voice. It was the same one he'd heard in the alley. He was sure of it. Suddenly, his heart was pounding and he was wet with perspiration.

"W-where are you?"

"I am where I always am, Mr. Stoker," the voice said. "In the shadows."

"What do you want?" Stoker shouted. His voice sounded abnormally loud. "Are you here t-to kill me?"

"Kill you?" The voice laughed, a low, rumbling laugh. "My word, no, not at all, Stoker. I am here to solicit your help."

"My help?" Stoker's tone was incredulous. "How can I help you?"

"Well, you can begin by continuing on to your office. Go on, keep walking. I'll be . . . along."

"T-to my office?"

"Yes," the man said. "Go, now!"

Stoker started walking, slowly at first, then more quickly, and then almost running.

He reached his door, opened it and entered. He almost expected to see someone seated inside, but that was not the case. There was, however, something on his desk. He hesitated, then approached, leaving the door open. Why lock it and annoy the killer by attempting to keep him out? After all, he was already in the building. Why anger him?

Stoker went around to the other side of his desk and sat down; his knees were weak. He could see two pages of a letter, written in an almost illegible handwriting, in red ink. The salutation read, "Dear Boss."

"Go ahead," the killer said from the hall, where he stood out of range of the lamp on Stoker's desk. "Read it. I need your opinion."

"My opinion?"

"Your professional opinion, as a writer," the man said. "I know the language is crude, but I am more interested in your thoughts."

Stoker looked down at the letter, but the words began to swim before him and, for a moment, he was afraid he would faint.

"W-what do you want to know?"

"Simply put," the man said, "I want to know if I make my point."

Stoker thought he could see a silhouette in the hall. A man with a top hat and dark clothing, perhaps even a cloak. He squinted but could not bring the image into sharper focus.

"The letter, Mr. Stoker," the man said. "I need you to keep your attention on the letter. If you're not going to help me, perhaps I *should* just kill you."

"No!" Stoker said, speaking too sharply. "No, I-I'll read it."

And so he did:

Dear Boss,

I keep on hearing the police have caught me but they wont fix me just yet. I have laughed when they look so clever and talk about being on the *right* track. That joke about Leather Apron gave me real fits. I am down on whores and I shant quit ripping them till I do get buckled.

Grand work the last job was. I gave the lady no time to squeal. How can they catch me now. I love my work and want to start again. You will soon hear of me with my funny little games. I saved some of the proper <u>red</u> stuff in a ginger beer bottle over the last job to write with but it went thick like glue and I cant use it. Red ink is fit enough I hope <u>ha. ha.</u> The next job I do I shall clip the ladys ears off and send to the police officers just for jolly wouldn't you. Keep this letter back till I do a bit more work, then give it out straight. My knife's so nice and sharp I want to get to work right away if I get a chance. Good Luck.

By the time he finished reading it he was able to decipher the handwriting well enough, and he was chilled to the bone. He was glad he'd left both pages lying side by side on his desk to read it. Holding it would have revealed the fact that his hands were shaking.

"So, what do you think?" the killer asked. "Not deathless prose, but it certainly reeks of death, eh?"

Stoker could only nod. Indeed, the letter was no

deathless prose, but he suspected that was deliberate. He had no doubt that the man he was speaking with now could have penned a much more literate letter—if he had wanted to.

The comment concerning Leather Apron referred to a story he had read in the newspaper, recounting that a man named John Pizer, also known as Leather Apron, was a suspect. This was obviously a source of amusement to the killer.

"And what do you think of the name I signed?"

Stoker looked at the second page. There, above a postscript to the letter, was the name the killer had apparently chosen to be known by.

Yours Truly,

Jack the Ripper
Dont mind me giving the trade name

PS Wasnt good enough to post this before I got all the red ink off my hands curse it No luck yet. They say I'm a doctor now. ha ha

"Well?"

Stoker looked up. He could now clearly see the outline of a figure standing in the hall. Definitely wearing a hat and cloak, the face hidden by the darkness. He seemed tall—as tall as Henry Irving?

He couldn't tell, but Irving and Stoker were the only two with keys to the theater. Had the killer gotten the key from Irving? Or . . .

"It fits you," Stoker said, aware that the man was awaiting a reply. "Jack."

"Yes," the killer said, " 'Jack the Ripper.' I thought it very fitting. So then you approve of my letter? As an author yourself, I mean."

"Does it accomplish what you want it to?" Stoker asked.

"Oh, my, yes," Jack the Ripper said.

"And where do you intend to send this?"

"Well," the Ripper said, "I had intended it for the police, but I would like it to go out to all the newspapers and telegraph services. I was hoping you could help me with that as well."

"Me? How?"

"Just a suggestion, Mr. Stoker," the Ripper said, "that's all I ask of you. In order to be sure this gets out—well, *everywhere,* where should I send it?"

This was preposterous. This murderer was asking him where to send the letter. If he told him, would this somehow make him an accessory to these murders?

"Come now, Mr. Stoker," Jack said. "No one will ever know of our visit tonight unless you tell them. And I will certainly never tell anyone that you commented on my letter and suggested where to send it. After all, I do want to appear . . . independent."

Stoker swallowed, found his voice. Despite feeling fear in the presence of the self-named Jack the

Ripper, he was also feeling something else—awe to be in the presence of someone so . . . so depraved. But was *depraved* even a strong enough word?

"Mr. Stoker?"

"I—" Stoker said, then stopped just a moment to catch his breath before continuing. "Well, I think perhaps it would be wise to send it to the Central News Limited."

"And that is?"

"An agency that would insure the letter went out to all the services you mentioned."

"And would they send it to the police?"

"I suppose that would depend on how responsible the editor there is."

"You know this fellow?"

"I do not," Stoker said.

"No matter. I can find his name. Yes, that is what I shall do. Thank you, Mr. Stoker, for your invaluable assistance."

"A-and now?" Stoker asked, his voice almost a croak.

"Hmm?" The Ripper seemed preoccupied. "Oh, you mean, am I going to kill you?"

"Uh, yes, that's—that's what I mean."

"No, no," Jack said. "You are my . . . let us call you my mentor, eh? When next I wish to write a letter or note to someone, I shall once again come to you for your council."

"I see."

"Would that be . . . all right with you?"

Stoker hesitated. Did he want to talk to the Ripper again, be in his presence again, experience this myriad of emotions he was now feeling again? Fear, loathing, yet awe and curiosity?

"Y-yes," Stoker said. "Yes, that would be . . . fine."

"But we must have some rules."

"Rules?"

"Oh, yes," Jack said, "rules will be very important if we are to have a relationship."

"And what would those rules be?"

The figure in the doorway moved, and Stoker thought for the first time that he saw the flesh of Jack's hands as the man gestured.

"Well, first you cannot go to the police. If you do, our association would be over and there would be . . . consequences. Understood?"

"Y-yes."

"Second, we will meet at times of my choosing, and always in the evenings."

"Evening?"

"Yes."

"You mean . . . after dark?"

"Yes."

"When the, uh, sun goes down?"

"That is usually when it becomes dark."

"Of course it is," Stoker said. "All right, then, times of your choosing."

"And places."

"Yes," Stoker said, "of course."

"Good. And third, you must never, ever make an

attempt to see my face. That would be a . . . a *fatal* error in judgment. Understood? And agreed?"

"Yes," Stoker said, "definitely both understood and agreed."

"Excellent."

"And, uh, is there another rule?"

"Not a rule," Jack the Ripper said, "but a suggestion."

"W-what would that be?"

"Bring your wife home, Mr. Stoker," Jack said. "I would never touch her. You have my word."

"You . . . know about my wife?"

"Oh, yes," Jack said. "I'm sure she loves her mother, but she has been there much too long, don't you agree?"

"Oh, yes, I do agree. Much too long."

"Good. Now extinguish your lamp, please. I would like to retrieve my letter from your desk."

"Oh, the letter . . . I could bring it, oh . . ." Stoker realized that taking the letter across the room to the Ripper was out of the question. It might even be misconstrued as an attempt to see Jack's face. And the Ripper coming into the room while the lamp still burned was equally out of the question.

"I will not harm you, Mr. Stoker," Jack said, as if reading Stoker's mind. "The lamp, please. It's time for me to go."

"Yes," Stoker said, "of course."

He reached out and plunged the room into darkness.

"Just sit still . . ." Jack said.

Stoker sat frozen. He heard a whisper of cloth, felt a breeze on his face, heard the rustle of paper, and then . . . nothing.

Jack the Ripper was gone.

Chapter Thirty-two

It took some time before Stoker could muster the nerve to light the lamp again. When he did he blinked, looked around and heaved a sigh of relief. Jack the Ripper was gone, and he was still alive. He looked down at his desk and saw that the letter was also gone.

He sat there for several moments, searching for some sign that he might have fallen asleep at his desk and dreamt the encounter, or perhaps had even suffered some sort of attack, hallucinated the entire thing. Ultimately, however, he had to admit that it *had* taken place. The proof, of course, would come if and when the letter appeared in the newspapers. But whether it did or not, the man had been here, and had christened himself Jack the Ripper.

There were several questions that sprang to mind. First, should Stoker go to the police and tell them? He had already given Inspector Swanson the name Jack. Should he now give him the full name of Jack the Ripper, or let the man discover it himself? And what of another meeting with Jack? That was certainly something the police would like to know about, but if they decided to have Stoker watched day and night, wouldn't that defeat Stoker's own purpose of trying to see inside the man? If Stoker aided in Jack's capture would the man talk to him while in captivity? And what of Florence? Could he risk her life by taking the word of a madman and asking her to return home?

Stoker rose and walked to his office door. He stopped there, listened intently, and then stepped into the hall. Instead of turning up the lights in the theater he simply fetched a torch and carried it down the hall with him. He stopped in front of Henry Irving's dressing room. There was a light shining from beneath the door where there had not been one before. Again, he chose to be still and listen before acting.

First, he had to shake off the feelings of betrayal he experienced for wondering if the man in the hall—Jack the Ripper—had indeed been Henry Irving in costume. If he entered Irving's dressing room now, would the man be seated in front of his mirror, in full Jack the Ripper garb? And how much would Jack resemble Mr. Hyde?

He turned the doorknob and pushed the door

open. The only light was at Irving's dressing table, but there was no one in the room. He entered and closed the door behind himself. There was a clothing rack to the left, where Irving kept his most often used costumes. It was Walter Collinson's job to keep the garments clean and ready for use. Stoker went to the rack and began to go through the clothing. About halfway through he found the cloak and suit worn by Irving when he played Mr. Hyde. He stopped and stared. Indeed, this certainly could have been the cloak worn by Jack the Ripper. He searched further, and atop the rack found Mr. Hyde's silk hat. There were many men in England who wore a cloak and a top hat, not just Mr. Hyde and Jack the Ripper. This proved nothing. However, combined with Irving's behavior of late and Collinson's bundles of clothing that had seemed to have blood on them, it was still cause for concern.

Stoker turned and sat in front of Irving's mirror. The tabletop was filled with glues and creams used in applying and removing makeup. Even Henry Hyde's sideburns were there, in a small box. What of Jack the Ripper? Did he have sideburns? A mustache?

This was preposterous. Jack had been there, outside his office, but Henry Irving was not Jack. Better to come to terms with the fact that he, Bram Stoker, now had a relationship of sorts with a mad mutilator and killer of women. The questions abounded in his head, coming fast and furious, still.

Keep this news to himself, or confide it to someone? Harker? Florence? Or Conan Doyle? Or someone new, like Oscar Wilde?

In the end he decided it needed to be someone not as easy to intimidate as Harker, nor as close to him as Florence, or as prone to flamboyance as Wilde. He left the theater—after checking that the doors were locked—and went in search of calm and coolly logical Arthur Conan Doyle.

He debated whether to go to Doyle's home first, or some of the clubs and pubs the man frequented. Wanting to avoid contact with Doyle's wife if possible, he went to several literary haunts he knew Doyle frequented. He found his friend surrounded by other literary cohorts in a pub on Arundel Street, between the Strand and the Thames, almost at the point where Fleet Street began. He had to feign coincidence and sit and drink with them for several hours before they all began to fade away and he was finally left sitting with Conan Doyle over a pint.

"Coincidence, indeed," Conan Doyle said when they were alone.

"Was I so transparent?"

"To me, yes, but I know you, sir," Conan Doyle said. "I could see you bursting with news to share but not daring to bring it up in the company of the others. Shall I assume, then, that this has to do with the Whitechapel killer?"

Stoker hesitated. Now was the time to share his experience, and he faltered. Would Conan Doyle think him mad, that he had imagined it all? There was only one way to tell, and that was to blurt it out.

"Jack the Ripper," he said, and then immediately looked around. His voice sounded impossibly loud to himself, even though he had spoken softly.

"Who?"

"That is his name," Stoker said. "It is what he calls himself. Doyle, I met him tonight, I spoke with him. I . . . I advised him."

Conan Doyle stared at his friend in shocked silence, and Stoker said the name once again.

"Jack the Ripper."

Chapter Thirty-three

Arthur Conan Doyle listened intently to Bram Stoker's account of his second meeting with the man who had declared himself to be Jack the Ripper.

When Stoker finished talking he drank the rest of his pint, which had gone warm. What he wanted, however, was the wetness.

"Doyle?"

Conan Doyle was sitting back in his chair, his mind taking in everything Bram Stoker had told him and turning it over, looking at it from every direction.

"Bram," he said, finally, "you believe that the man you spoke to in the theater tonight was actually the killer?"

"Yes, I do."

"You answered that with conviction."

"I *believed* him, Doyle," Stoker said. "I believe he was the same man who spoke to me in the alley that night, and I believe him to be the man he says he is—the man who killed all those women . . . Jack the Ripper."

"All right," Conan Doyle said, "and I believe you. The question is, what to do next."

"That's right," Stoker said.

"Stoker, you have an amazing opportunity here."

"To help the police catch him?"

Conan Doyle looked around to make sure no one else could hear them.

"You've got a book in your head, don't you? In the back of most writer's heads is *the* book. The one they are longing to do, and do right. You've got one, don't you?"

Stoker hesitated, then said, "Yes."

"And it has to do with . . . with this," Conan Doyle said, sitting back and spreading his hands. "With what has been going on."

"It has to do with the darkness of man," Stoker said.

"Then you know what I mean," Conan Doyle said. "You understand when I say this is a rare opportunity for you."

"I realize that," Stoker said. "I know I will never have the opportunity again to do this kind of research—but do I have the right?"

"Stoker the man is asking that," Conan Doyle

said. "What does Stoker the writer, the artist, think?"

"Stoker the artist," Bram Stoker said, "would do anything to be sure this book is done right."

Conan Doyle sat back in his chair and gave Stoker a look that spoke volumes.

Jack the Ripper followed Bram Stoker every step of the way from the Lyceum Theater until he reached the pub on Arundel Street. He was happy that the man never once made an attempt to contact the police. Apparently, he was looking for more than a pub to drink in; he was probably looking for someone to confide in—someone he could trust. That was fine with Jack. If Stoker was going to be of assistance to him, the man had to be comfortable—to a certain degree—with the relationship. If confiding in a friend helped bring that about, so be it.

Jack was satisfied that Stoker would not go to the police. If he were going to do that it would have been immediate. He felt sure of that. What he had felt pass between himself and Stoker was binding. They had a relationship now that was based on a mutual need. He did not know what Stoker's need was, but he knew it was there.

He knew he could go inside and find out who Stoker was talking to, but he did not think it was necessary. The bond between them was complete—and he had a letter to mail.

Chapter Thirty-four

By the evening of the September 29, the "Dear Boss" letter had still not appeared in any newspaper. Stoker began to wonder if the police had gotten hold of it and kept it from being reprinted in the news. He had no doubt, however, that Jack the Ripper had mailed it. He felt certain the Ripper would do what he said.

Stoker had spent the day battling ticket holders, assuring them that they would get their money's worth by holding on to them. For the most part he was successful, but there were those who demanded a refund, and he was forced to comply. The Lyceum coffers were getting lower by the day. But he knew that his efforts had been halfhearted, because his thoughts were more of Jack the Ripper than the problems of the theater. He wondered when he'd hear from the Ripper again, and despaired that it might be never. Now that he had this link with the killer he did not wish to lose it.

Harker had been doing his job and stayed away from Stoker for the most part. That night in the alley had apparently frightened him off for good. Stoker didn't know if the man was deliberately avoiding him or had simply been busy, but it really didn't matter. Their Holmes and Watson relationship was definitely over.

Stoker had convinced himself that the man who had come to him several nights earlier—Jack the Ripper—could not possibly have been Henry Irving. However, he had not yet discussed the possibility with Irving that he might have mislaid his keys to the theater. If he had not, then Jack the Ripper was either as good a burglar as he was a murderer, or he had entered the theater in some . . . supernatural method, perhaps the same way he had escaped that alley.

Once again, as he did night after night, Stoker made his rounds of the theater before he left for home. Even in the wake of Jack the Ripper's easy entry, old habits were hard to break. And good old-fashioned door locks would still keep petty thieves and burglars at bay.

He had collected his top coat from his office and was heading for the back door of the theater when he heard Henry Irving's dressing room door open. For some unfathomable reason he chose to secret himself in the shadows and watch. He thought it might be Walter Collinson leaving, but the figure he saw exit the room was neither Collinson nor Henry Irving. It appeared for all the world to be . . . Henry Hyde!

Stoker's amazement prevented him from reacting immediately. It gave Hyde time to leave the theater by the back door.

He hurried from his hiding place and made his way to the street. He looked up and down and saw the figure of Hyde heading away from the theater, rather than around toward the front of it. He felt he had no choice but to follow.

They walked several blocks before Hyde hailed a passing cab. The dark-cloaked figure climbed into the cab and gave the driver an address Stoker could not hear. Frantically, Stoker began to look for a cab of his own. He could hear the sounds of the cab's horse as it started down the street, and then suddenly there was an echoing sound as another cab pulled up the street from the opposite direction. He ran into the street, waving wildly until the driver reined his horse to a halt.

"Must be in pretty dire need of a lift, guv," the driver said.

"Another cab has left just ahead of us. If you hurry you can catch up to him."

"That's no problem, guv. Ol' Betsy here is the best horse on the streets of London—"

"Please, just go," Stoker implored. "I will tell you what I want as we go."

"As you please, guv." The driver started ol' Betsy off at a fast trot.

"I don't want you to catch up to the other cab," Stoker said. "Just get within sight of it and follow."

"Ah, I gets ya, guv," the man said. "Fella been 'aving it off wit' yer wife, is it?"

"Something like that," Stoker said.

"Ah, I knows how that feels. Been through it me-self. Don't worry, guv. We'll catch up and follow along. Fact is, I can 'ear 'im now. Sounds to me like 'Arry Folkke's mare, Annabelle. She can't outrun me own Betsy, 'at's fer sure."

The man proved to be right. It took only moments for them to come within sight of the other cab, and then they fell back, following from a safe distance.

"Don't worry, guv," the driver said. " 'Arry's almost deaf and won't 'ear us behind him."

Stoker only hoped that Henry Hyde wouldn't hear them either.

The fact that the figure had come from Irving's dressing room led Stoker to be fairly certain that they were following Irving dressed as Mr. Hyde. But why would he be going out into the streets in Hyde's clothing—and possibly even makeup? For what purpose?

They had followed along for some time when the driver turned and said, " 'Ere now, guv. Looks like they're headin' for Whitechapel. That ain't a place ta be goin' at night."

"Don't worry, my good fellow," Stoker said. "The

Ripper hasn't killed a cabbie yet. He's sticking to prostitutes."

"Who's that ya say?"

Stoker realized he'd slipped and called the killer the Ripper. He was still the only one who knew what the man was calling himself.

"Never mind. I'll double your fare," Stoker said, leaning forward. "Just don't lose them."

"For triple the fare I'll sticks ta them like glue, guv."

Stoker sat back and shouted, "Done!"

It was half past midnight when they reached White-chapel. Stoker's driver had fallen farther back as it was particularly deserted and quiet in the area and he didn't want to be seen or heard. Stoker feared that the man might have been deliberately trying to lose the first cab so that he would not have to drive into the Whitechapel area.

"You're going to lose them!" Stoker hissed urgently.

"Not at all, sir," the driver assured him, and then hastily jerked on ol' Betsy's reins to avoid colliding with the first cab as they came around a turn.

" 'Ere, wot's that? Wot're ya doin'?" the other driver called back. "Are ye daft? Is that you, Bill Tucker?"

"Aye, it's me, 'Arry. Yer stopped rather sudden-like—"

'Wot're ya doin' drivin' so close ta me, then?" Harry Folkkes shouted.

213

Before the two men could get into a full-fledged shouting match, Stoker stepped down and got between them.

"Where's your fare?" he shouted.

"Eh?" Folkkes replied. "Say again?"

"Your fare! Where did he go?"

"Damned if I know," Folkkes said. "He bid me stop suddenlike, paid me my fare and hopped out. Off at the run he went."

"Which way?"

The driver pointed almost aimlessly and said, "That way, I suppose."

As the two drivers began to bicker once again Stoker pushed money into Tucker's hand, easily three times what the fare should have been. He hurried off then, hoping to catch sight of Henry Hyde. But the man had obviously run off, perhaps knowing he was being followed.

Stoker began to move more urgently, not quite at a run but fast enough for his breath to come quicker. He stopped at one point and found himself standing at the base of a signpost that told him the name of the street he was on: WHITECHAPEL ROAD.

Chapter Thirty-five

Though only five-foot-five inches tall, Elizabeth Stride was known to most as Long Liz. Once a pretty woman, her face now held only a small remnant of her former self. To the man on whose arm she was hanging, though, that didn't seem to matter. She was simply the woman who was going to show him "a good time."

"Come along, lovey," she said in her most seductive voice. "I knows just the place for you and me to consummate our friendship, so to speak."

As she tugged the man down Berner Street Commercial Road she could hear the coins jingling in the rather large coin sack he'd shown her. Keeping hold of his arm with one hand, she reached between his legs with the other and found him hard and ready. She reasoned it wouldn't take her long to earn her money.

Of course, she had no idea that his excitement was of another kind entirely.

Stoker found himself wandering along the streets of Whitechapel. He turned away the advances of several prostitutes, wondering what they were doing on the streets this late, considering the recent actions of Jack the Ripper. Did they have no fear, or was it desperation that forced them to continue to ply their trade?

Stoker passed a coffee shop on Spectacle Alley and resisted the inviting smells coming from within. Somewhere on these streets Henry Irving might be wandering about as Henry Hyde, and Stoker was afraid that his boss—his friend—was not in his right mind. The last thing Irving needed was for some eager policeman to mistake him for Jack the Ripper.

Stoker realized quite suddenly that even while searching anxiously for Irving he could not help but feel some sense of pride at having been the first person Jack the Ripper had revealed himself to, by name.

" 'Ere we go, ducks," Long Liz said, opening the gate to Duffield's Yard. "Step into me office, as it were."

"After you, madam," Jack the Ripper said, rolling an open hand at the gate.

"Ooh, a gentlemen," Elizabeth Stride said.

"Don't find many of them around this part of town these days, luv."

She started ahead of him but was taken aback abruptly when Jack grabbed hold of her scarf and tugged it hard. She squawked for a moment, her eyes bugging out, and barely had time to panic before the blade kissed the skin of her neck, tearing it from ear to ear. Somehow she managed a scream— more of a loud squeal—and Jack decided there was too much risk involved in going any further with what he'd had planned for her. He eased Long Liz lovingly to the ground, dead, and melted into the shadows.

Stoker wandered about for a good half hour or more. He lost track of time as he zigzagged the dark Whitechapel streets in search of Irving. Should he give up, he wondered, or keep looking? If he left Irving to his own devices what would happen?

He decided to keep looking a little longer.

A half hour after Elizabeth Stride breathed her last, Catherine Eddowes never saw her end coming. The killer caught her from behind in Mitre Square and made his first cut while dragging her to the ground. She was drowning in her own blood by the time he had her down on the cobblestoned road. He was quick in his task, nearly flaying her face as he sliced her eyebrows and cut off the tip of her nose. By the time he made the incision in her abdomen, opening her from crotch to breast, she was dead.

Humming as he worked, he pierced her liver and sliced her navel, leaving it hanging on a tonguelike piece of skin. Happy with his progress, inhaling the scent of her intestines, licking drops of her blood that had spattered his lips and chin, he lifted her skirt and proceeded to cut her vagina and her rectum. This would be his best work to date, his most complete disemboweling of one of his women. . . .

He was almost finished when he heard footsteps approaching. He turned and saw a man. With a muttered curse at being interrupted when he was not quite ready to leave, he got to his feet and fled into the darkness. . . .

Stoker entered Mitre Square, wondering how he was going to find his way back to Whitechapel Road, when he saw the man crouched over what appeared to be the body of a woman. He froze momentarily, convinced he had stumbled across Jack the Ripper at work. But he quickly realized the dark, cloaked figure was Henry Hyde—in actuality, Henry Irving.

"Henry—" he said.

Irving looked up at Stoker as he approached. He had even donned the Hyde sideburns for his excursion.

"Bram," Irving said, his eyes wide with—what? Fear? Shock? Certainly the red-rimmed eyes of Henry Hyde. His hands, Stoker could see, had blood on them, as did his shirt and cloak.

"Henry, for God's sake . . ."

"Wha—" Irving said, then looked down at the woman and back at Stoker. "Nooooo . . . you can't think that I . . . you don't think . . . Bram, I didn't—"

Stoker made an immediate decision. He knew he wanted to get Henry Irving away from there. Even if he had killed the woman, he was most certainly not in his right mind when he had done the deed.

"Henry, come on," Stoker said, grabbing his friend's arm.

"But—but—her—" Irving said, as Stoker yanked him to his feet.

"Henry!" he said, forcefully. "We have to get away from here. Do you understand?"

"Y-yes . . . yes, I understand . . . but . . ."

"Henry, I need you to concentrate," Stoker said. "I'm lost; I'm turned around. I need you to focus, damn it!"

"All right . . . all right . . ."

"Do you know the way back to Whitechapel Road?"

"Yes," Irving said. "Yes, I do."

"All right," Stoker said, "then you have to get us there so we can hire a cab, and you have to get us there now!"

Chapter Thirty-six

By the time they arrived at the Lyceum it was Stoker who was in a panic. Irving appeared calm—too calm. They entered by the Burleigh Street door and made their way to Irving's dressing room in the dark. Once inside, Stoker lit a lamp and turned to Irving. In the small room his presence as Mr. Hyde was oppressive.

"For God's sake, take off that getup!" Stoker snapped. He could not remember ever before having spoken to Irving in such a tone. And yet the man reacted calmly, sat down in front of his mirror and began to disassemble Mr. Hyde, first wiping blood from his hands.

"Give me the cloak and the shirt," Stoker said,

"and anything else that has blood on it."

Irving obeyed and said, "Walter will wash them."

"Wash? They should be burned."

"No," Irving said, wiping his face with cream, "Walter has done it before."

"Before? Washed blood from your—of course." Stoker had been right those other times; it *had* been blood on the Irving's clothes. He bundled the cloak with the shirt inside and tossed them into a corner. Then he looked down and addressed Irving.

"Henry, we have to talk."

"Yes, I know." Irving continued to stare at himself in the mirror. The Hyde sideburns and eyebrows were gone. Also the wig. Stoker was now looking at his old friend, his mentor, Henry Irving.

"Henry, look at me."

Irving turned and regarded Stoker calmly.

"Did you kill that woman?" Stoker asked. "Or any of those other women?"

"No, of course not," Irving replied. "Don't be an ass, Bram."

"Wait, wait," Stoker said. "Don't go back to your makeup. What were you doing out there tonight dressed as Hyde?"

Irving studied Stoker's face for a few moments, then said, "I . . . I go out sometimes, at night, for a walk."

"A walk? As Henry Hyde?"

"Yes."

"Since when?"

222

"Since I started researching the part," Irving explained. "Even before the play opened I dressed as Hyde and went out. I would act in . . . in a lewd, abrasive manner toward people . . . women in particular . . . but I couldn't do it in respectable neighborhoods, so . . ." He shrugged.

"So you chose Whitechapel."

"Yes."

"But the killings had already started in Whitechapel. Why would you go there?"

Irving shrugged again. "The madman was killing women. What did I have to fear?"

"How about being mistaken for the madman?"

"That . . . never occurred to me."

Stoker stared at Irving for a moment. "You certainly looked the part tonight, Henry."

"I stumbled across that woman, Bram," Henry Irving said. "I was trying to see if I could help her, but she had been . . . mutilated. There was nothing I could do for her. And then you came along and . . . startled me."

"*I* startled *you?*" Stoker stared at Irving incredulously. "Henry . . ." Then he heaved a helpless sigh and asked, "Did you see anything? Anyone?"

"A man."

"You did?"

"Well . . . a figure, dressed in dark clothes."

"Like yours?"

"Like Hyde's, yes."

"Henry," Stoker said, "whatever is driving you to

go out as Mr. Hyde, it has to stop—*now*. It's over. We'll be going on to *Macbeth* as soon as we can."

Irving stared at Stoker, and then something happened to his face. It almost crumbled as he said, "I don't know what happened, Bram. I simply became . . . obsessed with the character. And then, when this killer started up in Whitechapel, I began to wonder . . . was he like Mr. Hyde?"

Worse, Stoker thought, much worse, but he didn't say anything.

"You've got to get over it, Henry," Stoker told him. "It's not safe, and it's not healthy."

"Yes, yes, Bram," Irving said, "you're right, of course."

"And Walter . . . he's been helping you with this? Encouraging you?"

"Helping, yes; encouraging, not at all," Irving said.

"Henry, about the blood . . ."

Irving misunderstood. He looked down at his hands and said, "Oh, I've gotten it off—"

"No, I mean . . . I saw Walter leaving with bloody clothing on two occasions, taking them to be . . . washed or burned?"

Irving looked at Stoker strangely, then said, "Well, washed, of course. Why would he burn—oh, I see. You thought it was the blood of those dead women."

"Well . . ."

"It's funny, really," Irving said. "The East End, all

those streets in disrepair, I wasn't used to it. I tripped and fell one night, scraped my arm up pretty good." He pulled back a sleeve, and Stoker saw an almost healed scab along his forearm. "I've kept it hidden all this time . . ."

"That explains one night," Stoker said. "What about the other?"

"The oth—oh, Fussie."

"The dog?"

Irving smiled. "She's a bitch, Bram, and she goes into heat once a month. One day she was tracking blood all over the dressing room and Walter grabbed the first thing he could find . . . a shirt."

Fussie's blood. Both instances of bloodied Irving clothing explained away logically. Stoker believed Irving—and realized what relief he felt.

"Walter did know about these . . . nights out, though."

Irving nodded. "He'll be very happy when I give it up."

"When exactly will that be, Henry?"

Irving reached for Hyde's sideburns and eyebrows, turned and dropped them into the trash.

"Now, Bram."

"Good," Stoker said. "Very good." He stood up. "I'm going to my office. Come by there when you're dressed and we'll go and get a drink."

"All right," Irving said. Stoker started for the door, but Irving stopped him. "Bram?"

"Yes."

"I didn't kill . . . I *never* killed anyone."

"If I didn't believe you, Henry," Stoker said, "I wouldn't have rushed you away from there."

Stoker went to his office and turned on his lamp. Lying on the desk was what looked like a letter written in red ink, and a note written in blue. He felt a thrill go through him—not fear, not anymore. He was a confidant of Jack the Ripper now, and as such had nothing to fear. He walked around the desk to read the handwritten note and the letter.

The note said:

> I did not have time to confer with you on this. It went in today's post. Do not feel slighted. I still need you.
> Jack
> P.S. The letter is a sample of the original, which was written on a post card.

The letter read:

> I was not codding dear old Boss when I gave you the tip, you'll hear about Saucy Jacky's work tomorrow double event this time number one squealed a bit couldn't

finish straight off. ha not the time to
get ears for police. thanks for keeping
last letter back till I got to work again
Jack the Ripper

Stoker examined the writing on the letter and the note and found them identical to that of the Dear Boss letter. There was no doubt in his mind that the same man had written them all.

What did Jack mean by a "double event"? he wondered. And he was calling himself Saucy Jack now. A nickname, perhaps?

Stoker heard footsteps in the hall approaching his door. They were Irving's; he could tell from the measured stride the man took with his long legs. Besides, if it had been Jack he simply would have appeared; Stoker would never have heard him. He knew that much about his new friend by now.

He hurriedly folded both notes and secreted them in a pocket. No time to look them over more carefully, or even read them again. He met Irving at the door, Jack the Ripper's newest missives burning holes in his pocket.

Chapter Thirty-seven

A pounding on Stoker's door awakened him abruptly on the morning of September 30. He staggered from his bed to the door and when he opened it found Arthur Conan Doyle standing there with a copy of *The Times* in his hands.

"It's true, by God!" he said, barreling into the house past Stoker.

"What's true?" Stoker asked, still only partially awake. He closed the door and turned to face his friend. He'd never seen Conan Doyle look so harried or unkempt before. He had obviously dressed in a hurry that morning, and had misbuttoned his vest.

"Shall I make us some tea?" Stoker asked.

"Damn the tea," Conan Doyle said. "Read this!"

He handed Stoker the newspaper. Stoker looked at the front, saw the words, "Dear Boss" and did not have to read any further.

"I know what it says," Stoker reminded Conan Doyle. "I told you what it would say."

"But it's true!" Conan Doyle said again. "Everything you told me about that night . . . it's true."

Stoker put his arm around Conan Doyle's shoulder and said, "Come. I think we both need some tea."

Some time later they were sitting in the kitchen, each with a cup in front of him. Conan Doyle had rebuttoned his vest and regained his composure, somewhat.

"So you didn't believe me when we spoke the other night," Stoker said.

"I did," Conan Doyle said. "I believed you, but . . . it's still fascinating to see it actually in print, isn't it?"

"Well," Stoker said, looking down at the paper, "don't forget that I saw it written in his own handwriting."

"Oh, yes, of course," his friend said. "I'm, uh, sorry . . . but . . . have you decided what you are going to do?"

"I'm not going to the police," Stoker said. "That may be irresponsible, but to be honest I doubt they would believe me."

"Well, the letter has already appeared in the newspapers. It's not as if you told them beforehand what it would say—as you did me. If you had they'd be as amazed as I am right now."

"I agree," Stoker said.

They drank their tea in silence for a few moments, each of them occasionally letting his eyes drift to the newspaper on the table between them. Stoker wondered why the newest murder had not yet been reported. He decided to keep that knowledge to himself for the time being, as well as the sample of the newest note Jack the Ripper had sent to the Central News Limited.

"What have you decided to do about Florence?" Conan Doyle asked, finally breaking the silence.

"I think I will leave her to her mother for a while longer," Stoker said. "I'm not quite ready to take the word of a murderer assuring me of her safety."

"He knew she was at her mother's," Conan Doyle pointed out thoughtfully.

"Your point being?"

"Do you think he knows where her mother lives?"

"I choose to believe not," Stoker said with a slight shudder. "If he does, however, then it really doesn't matter if I leave her there or bring her back here."

"That's true."

"What would you do now, Doyle?" Stoker asked. "I mean, if you knew that this murderer, this Jack the Ripper, could appear on your doorstep at any time."

"My dear friend," Conan Doyle said, "I think I would be beside myself with glee if I were the one he chose to appear to, rather than you. I would simply wait for him to show up again."

"I don't suppose there's much else I can do."

After Conan Doyle finished his tea and left, Stoker wondered if he should have told his friend about the other notes. He decided that perhaps he had been too free right from the beginning in taking people into his confidence—first Harker and then Conan Doyle. From this point on perhaps what passed between him and Jack the Ripper would stay with the two of them.

He went to his bedroom and removed the two notes from his jacket pocket. He reread the postcard note. "Thanks for keeping the last letter back till I got to work again." Stoker had no doubt that the first letter had probably been considered a hoax, and passed on to the police only after much thought. Even more thought must have gone into printing it.

No doubt tomorrow's newspapers would have the story of what happened last night, and perhaps even the postcard Jack the Ripper had sent.

Stoker wondered if Jack wasn't becoming too bold in his actions. He hoped that he would have the opportunity to talk to the Ripper again, spend more time with him, ask questions, before the police finally closed in on him.

Chapter Thirty-eight

Jack was concerned.

He knew Henry Irving had been wandering about Whitechapel last night dressed as Mr. Hyde. He also knew that only Bram Stoker's quick thinking had kept the police from catching Irving. He'd watched from the shadows as the actor and writer had confronted each other over the body of Catherine Eddowes, and as Stoker had dragged the bloodstained Irving away from the scene. Had the police captured Irving, the actor would surely have been arrested and charged as the killer, thereby stealing Jack's thunder. It was only Stoker's quick thinking, and admirable display of loyalty, that had saved the day.

On the other hand, Jack was very happy to see his letter in the newspapers before reports of the two women he had claimed as his own got out. He'd hoped the letter would appear sooner, but this was still acceptable. Tomorrow's tabloids would have the stories of the two women he'd taken in one night—a bold move, he knew, and one he was proud of. He hoped they would also carry the text of his latest missive, the Saucy Jack postcard.

However, while all of that was going according to plan, it was time for him to have a longer meeting with his new friend, Bram Stoker. He sat at the writing desk in his room, took blue ink to paper and wrote the note he would have delivered to the Lyceum Theater that day by one of his runners.

Chapter Thirty-nine

"Life's but a walking shadow, a poor player that struts and frets his hour upon the stage and then is heard no more; it is a tale told by an idiot, full of sound and fury, signifying nothing!"

The voice startled Stoker from his reverie. He must have come in from stage right, for there he was, center stage, reciting lines from *Macbeth* as if born to it.

"Are you impressed?" Jack asked.

He was shrouded in darkness. Stoker, whose eyes were fairly well adjusted, could still not make out much beyond a silhouette.

"Very," Stoker said.

"Delivered with the power of a Henry Irving?" Jack asked.

Stoker hesitated a moment, then decided to be as honest as he could in his relationship with Jack the Ripper.

"Not quite."

The Ripper laughed, the sound echoing across the stage and giving Stoker a chill.

"Good," he said, "very good. Stay honest with me, Stoker, and we shall continue to get along."

"Is that what you wanted to tell me?" Stoker asked. "Why we're meeting here tonight?"

"No," Jack said, pacing, enjoying the sound of his footsteps on the hard wood. "I like it up here."

Stoker realized how Jack was avoiding the stage left light.

"And I enjoy Shakespeare."

"Performing, or watching?" Stoker asked.

"Both, actually. In fact, I've been here on occasion to watch your Henry Irving perform."

For weeks the newspapers had been trying to determine what Jack's background, his place in society, must be. Was he highborn or lowborn, educated or uneducated, affluent or poor? Stoker now felt uniquely qualified to conjecture on the subject. He felt certain that no uneducated, lowborn, poverty-stricken soul had ever passed through the doors of the Lyceum Theater. For the Ripper to quote from *Macbeth*, and for him to have attended performances at the theater, meant he was definitely a man from a higher station in life.

"Perhaps you would like to, uh, sit?" Stoker offered.

"In the audience with tha?" Jack asked. "No, no, we must keep our distance, Bram. Our relationship depends quite heavily on you never seeing my face. Besides, I like it up here. It's . . . a heady experience, isn't it? I can see why Irving loves it so. Have you been up here, Stoker? Have you ever aspired to perform on the stage?"

"I am content to manage the theater for Irving," Stoker said.

The Ripper stopped moving about and turned to look at Stoker.

"Ah, yes, of course, your art is literary, not performance. Tell me, who do you count among your friends?"

"Well, I—"

"Oscar Wilde, I'll wager," the Ripper said. "Robert Louis Stevenson?"

"You've read *Jekyll and Hyde?*" Stoker asked.

"But of course," Jack said. "It's a work of genius, don't you think?"

"Well, yes, but—"

"It's a wonderfully depraved description of a man's descent into . . . what shall we call it . . . mental degeneration? Fascinating."

"Yes," Stoker said, "I agree."

Suddenly the Ripper came as close to Stoker as he dared, his hands the only part of his body visible.

"But that was fiction," he said, his tone becoming almost a purr. "What do you think? Can such a thing really happen to a man? Eh?"

Stoker felt as if he were being tested. Did the

Ripper actually want him to call him a madman? Did he want that much honesty between them?

"I have no doubt," Stoker said, carefully, "that men can become . . . obsessed—"

"Are we talking about me now, or your Henry Irving's obsession with Mr. Hyde?"

Stoker stared at the man shrouded in shadow.

"Oh, yes," Jack said. "I know about that. I know he was in Whitechapel last night, and even before then. I also know that you whisked him away before the police could come."

"H-how many women did you kill last night?"

Jack backed up, returned to the center of the stage. Stoker sensed the man's back was to him, and this was confirmed when he started to speak.

"Two women were killed last night, but what if I told you I only killed one of them," Jack said.

"What?"

"Who would you think killed the other?"

"Wait . . ." Stoker said, stunned.

"I am asking you," Jack said carefully, "who would you think killed the other one if I had only killed one of them?"

"No," Stoker said.

"No?"

"You are trying to make me think that Irving, dressed as Hyde, killed one of those women."

There was no reply.

"Jack?"

Silence. Stoker squinted but could no longer make out the shadowy figure on the stage.

"Not *dressed* as Hyde," Jack's voice said in his ear.

Stoker tried to leap from his seat, but Jack laid one hand on his shoulder, which was enough to deter him. The man's strength was amazing.

"Not dressed as Hyde," Jack said again, "and not even *acting* as Hyde."

The man's warm, fetid breath on Stoker's ear had a chilling effect.

"You're saying . . . that Irving *was* Hyde? That when he goes out *dressed* as Hyde he *becomes* Hyde?"

"I am asking," Jack said, "if you think that it is possible."

Suddenly Jack's hand disappeared. Stoker could not help himself. He leapt from his seat and turned, prepared to finally see the face of Jack the Ripper. No one there.

"Well?"

Jack was back at center stage.

"Henry didn't kill anyone!" Stoker shouted. "He couldn't."

"It's in every man to kill, Stoker," Jack the Ripper said. "Believe me, I know."

Finally, an opening to ask a question pertinent to his research.

"Was it always in you to kill?"

"Always," the Ripper replied. "As it is in tha."

"I don't want to kill anyone."

"Not now," the Ripper said. "But the time could come."

"As it came to you?"

Suddenly Jack dropped down into a crouch, as if he were considering his reply.

"It was awakened in me," he said. "It could awaken in any man, at any time."

"Awakened by what?" Stoker asked.

"I'm not sure," the Ripper replied. "One morning I just knew that this was what I had to do."

"So you are compelled to kill these women?" Stoker asked, trying to hide his excitement. "It's not something you *want* to do, but something you feel you *must* do?"

Jack hesitated, then said, "In all of us there are the things we aspire to do. Dream about. Long for. But the things we must do—but the things we are driven to do *must* take precedence."

Stoker could not believe he was actually getting Jack to talk about his reasons for killing the women. This was invaluable research for his book, a look inside the mind of a killer.

But in the next moment, the "interview" took a turn.

"For instance," Jack said, standing and moving slowly across the stage, "there is something compelling you now—something that has been compelling you for the past few weeks to seek me out, to walk in my tracks . . . something that compels you to ask these questions, to try to get inside me."

Stoker felt a coldness in his stomach. The man knew what he was thinking.

"What do you mean?"

"You are a writer, Stoker," Jack the Ripper said, "so you are being compelled to write something."

"By the same token, are you saying you are a killer who is compelled to kill?" Stoker asked. "You must be something other than a killer."

"I suppose there is something that I do—a path I used to walk—before I started on this one. But I am not so gormless as to speak further about myself. I want to talk about your book."

"What book?"

"The one you can't stop thinking about," Jack said. "The one that haunts you. The one you think will benefit if you could only find out what drives a mad killer such as myself."

Does a mad killer know he is one? Stoker wondered. And if he knows it, is he then still mad?

"I see you have many more questions to ask," Jack said. His voice came from stage right. "But are you sure they are questions about me and not about yourself?"

Suddenly the words seemed to echo from the darkness. It was as if Jack had left the stage and somehow moved into the rafters. His voice seemed to rise out of the darkness of the theater.

"Wait, Jack! Don't leave."

"We'll speak again, Stoker. Read the newspapers tomorrow. Learn what I did last night."

"But wait. You never said . . . did you kill both women?"

"That remains for next time," Jack said, his voice now a whisper, seemingly coming from inside Stoker's own head. "Until then, ask some questions of yourself, Bram Stoker. But be prepared for what you get."

Then, from the rafters, *"Tomorrow, and tomorrow, and tomorrow, creeps in this petty pace from day to day to the last syllable of recorded time, and all our yesterdays have lighted fools the way to dusty death!"*

Stoker returned to his office to extinguish his desk lamp and fetch his top coat. As he came around the desk, which was still covered with remnants of his research on Vlad the Impaler—notes and open books strewn across it—he noticed, written across one of the pages in large red letters the word *DRACULA.*

Chapter Forty

The following day the newspapers carried stories of the newly named Jack the Ripper's two latest victims. While the killer seemed to have had no time but to cut the first victim's throat and leave her for dead, he appeared to have had sufficient time to commit sorts of atrocities on the second. From all of this the press inferred two things: one, that the killer was now out of control. How else could it be explained that he had killed two women in one night, forty-five minutes apart? And two, that the police had no chance of ever catching him. The Ripper himself was so sure of this that he had gone out and killed two women in one night just to make his point.

The papers also carried the contents of the Saucy

Jack postcard. They declared that since the postcard was dated *before* the night of the two murders—effectively *predicting* them—it was obviously genuine.

Articles and editorials appeared calling for action by someone—*anyone*—to try to catch this maniac.

The name Jack the Ripper was spread across the front of every newspaper, to the satisfaction of two men—two very different men.

But were they really so different, after all?

Jack the Ripper was experiencing great satisfaction at all the attention he was receiving. His name would no doubt now be known throughout London, and perhaps all over Britain. Jack the Ripper was now famous—or, he thought, with an even higher degree of satisfaction, *infamous.*

He sat at his writing desk, staring down at copies of *The Morning Advertiser, The Telegraph, The Times* and even *The Financial News.* All of the London periodicals—large and small—were carrying his name on the front page.

Soon he would be the most famous person in British history.

Bram Stoker could not help but feel some satisfaction—indeed, pride—at the fact that it was he the killer had confided in. He had been the first to learn the name Jack the Ripper.

Stoker decided to read the morning newspapers seated at an outdoor café on the Thames before going to the theater. He drank his tea and carefully went through each story. Only the quality of the reportage changed from the larger tabloids to the lesser known, not the facts. According to the newspaper, the police had no doubt that both murders were the work of the man who had introduced himself as Jack the Ripper.

He put the newspaper down and stared out over the Thames. Jack had asked the night before what if he hadn't killed both women—but he had. He must have, for the alternative was unthinkable. Jack had been playing with him, trying to make him think Irving, as Hyde, was capable of murder. He had no doubt this was a ploy by Jack to keep himself in control of their relationship. Stoker—who wanted badly for the relationship to continue—was going to have to figure out a way to change that.

Stoker's desk and appearance had one thing in common—once neat and fastidious they were now both . . . unkempt. His beard, bushy but always carefully trimmed, had become something almost wild and forgotten, like an untended garden. His clothes were wrinkled, as if he'd slept in them. Without Florence around he was helpless when it came to something like laundry. He had taken to wearing the same shirt two, perhaps even three times, changing only the collar. They did not have a full-time maid in their house, and the one they had came in once a week to clean the house, but not to do laundry. Stoker had finally convinced her one day to do it by offering her some extra money. Already, though, he was beginning to run out of shirts again.

Even his work at the theater was suffering, for now all his waking hours—and some of the sleeping ones, as well—were filled with thoughts of Jack the Ripper, and what his relationship with a mad killer might mean to his book.

He sat at his desk, now not only covered with books and notes but with newspapers from the past two days. Pushing several of the periodicals to the side, he uncovered that scrawled red word: *DRACULA*. This was certainly Jack the Ripper's way of showing that he had been here, in what was once Stoker's sanctum sanctorum. Another attempt to establish his dominance.

The scrawled Dracula sent him back to his research. While the words *Vlad the Impaler* had become etched in his mind, the word *Dracula* had not. Now, directly on the page on which Jack had scrawled the name, Stoker was reminded that this was, indeed, the name by which Vlad was known. Stoker sat back and repeated the word in his mind a few times before actually saying aloud, "Dracula."

The name appealed to him. It had a dark, chilling quality to it, more chilling than even *the Impaler,* for some reason. What had Jack been trying to tell him? Had he chosen the word at random to scrawl in red—in blood—on the page? Or had he deliberately chosen the name to try to send a message to Stoker?

He was yanked from his thoughts when the door

to his office opened after a single perfunctory knock. He was surprised when Inspector Donald Swanson entered. As nonchalantly as he could, Stoker closed the book containing Jack the Ripper's message.

"Inspector," Stoker said, "good morning—or perhaps it isn't such a good one."

"I see you've been readin' the papers, like everyone else," Swanson said, approaching the desk.

"Indeed I have," Stoker said. "It is not the sort of thing one can miss, is it?"

"Do you mind if I sit?"

"Please," Stoker said. "Can I send someone for tea?"

Swanson was in the act of sitting when he arrested the movement and straightened.

"Perhaps we could go out, Mr. Stoker. Allow the Metropolitan Police to buy you a cup of tea."

"Well . . ."

"There is something I could use your help with, sir," Swanson said. "I think it would be better discussed . . . somewhere outside the theater."

Stoker studied the man for a few moments, wondering what he could have on his mind, then said, "Well, how could I resist such an invitation, then?"

Chapter Forty-one

They stopped in at a small tearoom a few blocks from the theater, led there by Swanson, who seemed to have the place in mind the whole time. The inspector ordered a pot and some scones, waiting until they were placed in front of them on the table to get to the business at hand. He filled the time with idle chatter about the theater and when Stoker thought they might be "up and running" again.

"We almost have everything in place for *Macbeth*," Stoker replied. "I only hope we have enough ticket holders to make putting on the production worth our while."

The inspector did not rise to the bait, and finally their tea and scones arrived.

"You're probably wondering what it is I think you can help me with," Swanson said.

"I'm very curious, yes."

"I'll get right to the point, then," the policeman said. "We have several reports of men who were seen on the streets of Whitechapel last night around the time of the two murders."

"That sounds promising," Stoker said. "Are they . . . good descriptions?"

"Well, there are some similarities that match other reports we've received. . . . For instance, a darkly dressed man, possibly wearing a cloak or a cape, with a top hat . . . Rather well dressed for that area of the city, but no descriptions beyond that, however."

"I see."

"No, you don't," Swanson said, "but I'm going to endeavor to make sure you do."

Stoker sipped his tea and set it down. He was pleased that his hand did not reflect the shaking he felt inside.

"You see, one of the people this description could fit is . . . well, Mr. Hyde."

"Inspector—"

"Or someone dressed as Mr. Hyde."

"Do you still think this Jack the Ripper is trying to emulate a fictional chara—"

"No," Swanson said, interrupting him, "I was thinking of someone else."

"Who—" Stoker began, but then he realized where the policeman was going with this. "Good

Lord, you can't be serious. You can't possibly be speaking of . . . Henry Irving? Inspector, I thought we had put this matter to rest—"

"I have put nothing to rest, sir," Swanson said harshly. "The women of Whitechapel—the women of London, for that matter—have not been able to rest since this barbaric business began." He leaned forward. "Was Henry Irving in Whitechapel last night?"

"No," Stoker said, making his first blatant lie to the police—but certainly not his last.

At breakfast that morning Donald Swanson's wife had said, "Darling, is something wrong with your breakfast? Shall I have Henrietta prepare something else for you?"

"Hmm?" Swanson looked across the table at his wife. Never a pretty woman, at forty she had developed into quite a handsome one. He was always proud to be seen with her on his arm. "Oh, no, dear, the breakfast is fine. It's this blasted case."

Swanson had been called out of bed at two A.M. to go to Whitechapel, and had only returned home in time for a two-hour nap, a change of clothes and some tea and toast.

"It's horrible," she said. "Two more women killed, and no one saw anything?"

"Someone did see something," Swanson said, "and that is what is bothering me. I have to go and see Mr. Stoker again, about Henry Irving."

"Surely you don't suspect either of those gentlemen?" she asked. "They are so respected in their fields—"

"I know," he said, cutting her off, "and they have the P.M.'s ear." He was referring to the current Prime Minister, Archibald Primrose, who had succeeded William Gladstone in 1886. Some predicted Gladstone would soon be reclaiming the office. "Luckily, he's a politician who likes to remain uninvolved as much as he can. You're right, of course, about Stoker and Irving, but . . . I can't shake the feeling he is lying to me."

"Henry Irving?"

He shook his head. "Bram Stoker. But he might be lying to *protect* Irving." The events in the Whitechapel alley that had resulted in four dead villains still rankled Swanson. Stoker knew *something*, of that he was sure. But what?

"I think the very idea is preposterous!" she announced. "Suspecting a marvelously talented actor like Henry Irving."

"I am sorry, my dear," Swanson said, dabbing at his mouth with a cloth napkin, "but it is my job to suspect everyone." He stood up.

"Donald! You haven't even finished your tea."

"I must get going, my dear," he said, moving to her side of the table and kissing the top of her head. "I am going to talk to Mr. Stoker, and if I believe he is lying to me . . . well, P.M. or no P.M., I'll have him up on charges!"

* * *

"I know for certain that Irving was in the theater until late last night," Stoker said.

"So that would mean you were also in the theater last night?" the policeman asked.

"That is correct."

"How late might it have been?"

"Henry and I were the last to leave," Stoker said, pausing a moment to make it seem as if he were trying to recall. "It was well on toward one A.M."

"One A.M.," Swanson said. "You're sure of that?"

"Fairly sure."

"That would not be because you read in the newspapers that the two murders had taken place between one and two?"

"Are you calling me a liar, Inspector?"

"Not at all," Swanson said. "I just thought that perhaps your recollection might have been . . . influenced by what you had read this morning."

"I assure you it was not."

"Very well, then," Swanson said. "One o'clock."

"Toward one, I said," Stoker said. "I would not say we were still in the theater at one."

"It doesn't really matter, does it?" Swanson asked. "You've not given yourself or Irving time to get from the theater to Whitechapel, have you?"

"Should I have?" Stoker asked. "Or should I apologize for not having done so?"

"Tell me, Mr. Stoker," Swanson asked, "why then do I have a description of a well-dressed man with a red beard apparently rushing away from the scene with another well-dressed man whose description resembles Mr. Hyde?"

"Or Jack the Ripper."

"Very well, either man. However, my question is keyed more upon the description of a red-bearded man."

Stoker touched his beard without meaning to, then rushed to try to overcome the possible blunder.

"Am I the only red-bearded man in London, Inspector?"

"I think you know you are not."

"Very well," Stoker said. "Then while admittedly I fit the description you've given, so do many other men."

"But none who are already involved."

"Involved . . . in what?"

"In the Jack the Ripper case."

"Good Lord," Stoker said, "when did I become 'involved' in that, pray tell? Are you insinuating that I am a . . . a suspect?"

Swanson sat forward, his anger barely controlled.

"I would say you became involved when you decided to tell your first lie, Mr. Stoker."

"And when would that have been, Inspector?"

Swanson stood quickly, upsetting his unfinished cup of tea, which fell to the floor, shattering and splashing his own shoes.

"I don't know that for certain, Mr. Stoker," the policeman said, "but I intend to find out."

Chapter Forty-two

For the next two weeks the newspapers demanded that the police do something about Jack the Ripper. Other letters appeared in the papers, but they were all thought to be hoaxes.

Bram Stoker knew for a fact that they were all fakes. He knew how Jack the Ripper sounded, both in person and in print. He also knew that Jack would come to him before he wrote another note, or letter, or postcard.

Days after his conversation with Jack that night in the theater, Stoker realized something. First, Jack had used some words that Stoker was not familiar with. On two occasions he'd referred to Stoker as *tha* rather than *you*, and had said something about being *gormless*. Stoker had never heard these words before. Jack was usually very well spoken, but perhaps those words were regional, and finding out where they were used might point to where Jack either lived or came from. Stoker had to find someone to ask.

Second, Jack had been calm—calm, serene, satisfied. Killing those two women in one night had apparently fulfilled him more than any of the other murders had. The police were now predicting the Ripper's murders were going to start coming closer together. They cited the two murders within an hour of each other as an indication that he was out of control.

Bram Stoker knew that was not the case. Jack the Ripper was anything but out of control, and Stoker felt that he would not need to kill another woman for some time. The fact that there were no murders over the next two weeks bore him out. What he wondered was, when would Jack need to speak with him again?

In addition to a rash of fraudulent letters and notes, the Whitechapel Vigilance Committee, under the leadership of one George Lusk, demanded that a reward of five hundred pounds be offered for information leading to the capture of Jack the Ripper. The request—presented in the form of a petition—was being firmly rejected by the Home Office of the Metropolitan Police. Lusk attempted to get his petition to Her Majesty the Queen, but instead was turned away by the Secretary of State for the Home

Department. However, the request did manage to garner publicity for the Vigilance Committee, and for Lusk himself.

On the evening of October 14 Stoker was locking up the Lyceum Theater. Over the course of the past two weeks he had been staying later and later, in the hope that Jack the Ripper would contact him. Staying late, however, did not mean he was keeping up with his work. In fact, performances of *Macbeth* might have already been underway had he been doing his job properly during that time. Instead he was letting matters slide, forgetting to make appointments, or to keep them once made. His office was becoming more and more of a mess, with theater business pushed to one side and newspaper piles growing larger and larger. Continued research into Vlad the Impaler's life was taking up more and more of his time. Once the purpose of his research had been to understand more about Jack the Ripper, but now he wanted to understand Vlad, wanted more insight into the legend of the vampire.

He sat behind his desk, pondering the name again, when he heard someone walking outside his office. It could only have been one of two people there that late—Henry Irving or Jack the Ripper.

He waited and listened, wondering if the footsteps would come directly to his door, but they did not. He left his chair and went out into the hall. Then to the theater itself to see if anyone was there—perhaps on stage, like last time?—but no one was.

He started to return to his office but was stopped by someone calling—or whispering—his name.

"Stoker."

"Who is it?"

"You know who it is," the disembodied voice said.

Stoker looked around himself in vain but could see no one. Here and there an electric light shone, casting shadows on the walls. But past experience had taught him that the speaker could have been in those shadows, or anywhere above him.

"Jack?"

"At your service."

"Where are you?"

"Close enough for you to hear me," the Ripper said.

"What do you want now?"

The Ripper's laugh sent a chill through him.

"Don't take that tone, Bram," the man said, "not when we both know you have been eagerly waiting for me to contact you again."

Stoker dropped the impatient act. "What is it, then? Another victim?"

"Another letter," Jack said, "and a surprise."

"A surprise?"

"The letter first."

"All right," Stoker said. "Where is it?"

"In Irving's room, on his dressing table."

"What were you doing in there?"

"I wanted to sit in the great thespian's chair. How is he these days? Still obsessed with Hyde?"

"No," Stoker said, "that's over with. Especially after . . . that night."

"Good," the Ripper said. "I won't need to chance tripping over him."

"You won't. He's concentrating on *Macbeth*."

"That performance should already be underway," Jack said. "What's the holdup?"

"It's been . . . difficult."

The Ripper laughed again, and Stoker waited for the echo of it to die down.

"I am taking you away from your work, aren't I, Bram?" he asked. "You've been obsessing about your book. The theater work suddenly seems . . . trivial, doesn't it?"

Stoker did not want the killer to know that he was right.

"Who are you sending this note to?" he asked.

"Go to Irving's room and read it," the Ripper said. "Then we will talk."

"Where will you be?"

The Ripper's laugh came for a third time. "I will be . . . near."

Stoker walked to Irving's dressing room and found the door unlocked. He entered. There was a single candle burning on the dressing table. Lying next to the candle was the note. Stoker knew Jack was making a statement by leaving it there, proving nowhere was off limits to him.

He sat down and read:

From Hell.
Mr. Lusk,
Sor
I send you half the Kidne I took from one woman and prasarved it for you tother piece I fried and ate it was very nise. I may send you the bloody knif that took it out if you only wate a whil longer
signed
Catch me when you can Mishter Lusk

Stoker read the note a second time before he remembered that the name of the man in charge of the Whitechapel Vigilance Committee was George Lusk.

"Why is the spelling so poor?" he wondered aloud. It was even worse than it had been in the first two missives.

"I prefer it that way."

He turned quickly; the voice had been so close, but he saw no one. It was as if Jack was invisible—or perhaps hiding behind the rack of costumes.

"Why?" he asked.

"It amuses me to let them believe I am less educated than I am," Jack said. "Also, it will confuse them."

"They'll think it's a hoax, like the others."

"Ah, the others," the Ripper said. "You knew they were fake?"

"Of course."

"Good. They will know this one is real because of . . ." He dropped his voice to a dramatic whisper as he said, ". . . the kidney."

"Are you really sending him a kidney?"

"Yes," the Ripper said in his usual tone. "One I borrowed from Catherine Eddowes. But I'm sure she won't mind."

"Why show me this, then? You don't want me to correct it, or critique it."

"I've come to think of you as a confidant, Bram," Jack said. "May I call you Bram?"

"Of course." Briefly, Stoker entertained the thought of springing up and sliding the clothes aside. However, all that might have gotten him was a slit throat.

"I feel . . . good about having someone to show these to before I post them. It brings me . . . closer to you."

Stoker opened his mouth to speak, but he was too dry. He summoned up as much saliva as he could to moisten his mouth and said, "That's good."

"Do you feel close to me, as well, Bram?"

"Yes." *Close* was not the word he would have chosen, but he could think of no other reply.

"Good," the Ripper said. "Then I feel justified in arranging a surprise for you."

"The surprise," Stoker said, reminded of it.

"What is it?"

"Ah," Jack said, "if I told you it would not be a surprise, would it?"

"I suppose not," Stoker said. "Look, I want to talk to you—"

"Another time," Jack said, the voice becoming fainter. "We'll talk another time, Bram. . . ."

"Jack." When there was no answer he called out again, more sharply. "Jack!"

No answer.

Stoker rose and walked to the door, which had been open the entire time. Could Jack have simply slipped out? He turned and looked at the rack that held Irving's wardrobe. Slowly, he approached it, reached out and slid the clothing aside, enabling him to look behind. All he saw was a blank wall. He was not sure whether or not what he felt was relief.

He went back to Irving's dressing table and looked at the note. It had been written in blue ink. He opened a drawer where he knew Irving kept matches. Tearing the note into pieces, he watched it burn in the brass ashtray. He wondered if Lusk would believe this note to be genuine and take it to the police, or to the newspapers.

When the paper had been reduced to a pile of ashes Stoker blew out the candle and left the dressing room. Walking back to his office, he knew Jack was gone. He could feel it.

As certain as he had been that the Lyceum was empty when he left it, Stoker was immediately aware that someone was in his house the instant he walked over the threshold.

"Hello?"

There was a light in the bedroom. He walked to the door and found Florence lying in bed, reading by the oil lamp they kept on the night table.

"Hello, darling," she said, laying the book down in her blanketed lap.

"Florence." He didn't know what else to say.

"Is that how you greet your wife after so long?" She extended her arms to him.

He walked to the bed, sat down next to her and kissed her warmly.

"Why do you look so surprised, my love?" she asked, hugging him.

"Well . . . I didn't know you were coming home."

She pushed him to arm's length and studied his face.

"You're joking, aren't you?"

"No," he said, "why should I be joking?"

"Darling, you sent me a note at my mother's telling me to come home . . . didn't you?"

"Where is this note?"

"On top of the dresser."

He stood up, walked to the dresser and picked up the note. It was short and to the point.

Come home, I miss you.

It was signed: *Bram.*

She came up behind him, put a hand on his arm. "Bram?"

"Didn't you notice that the handwriting is not mine?"

"I did . . . but who else could it have been from?"

He turned and looked at her. She was staring at him intently, waiting for an explanation. He wondered how he was supposed to tell her that she'd received a note from Jack the Ripper.

Chapter Forty-three

They were seated across from each other in the kitchen, each with a steaming cup of tea. As hot as it was, however, it did nothing to warm the chill his words left hanging in the air as he told her everything that had happened before she left, and since.

When he was done they sat in silence, trying to warm their hands with their cups. He waited patiently for her to find the words she would use to call him seven kinds of idiot—and he would not be able to argue with her. She would never understand what this book, this opportunity, meant to him—

"I understand," she said finally.

"What?" He was stunned. He'd expected to receive a tongue-lashing of epic proportions.

She smiled at him, reached across the table to take his hand.

"Do you think I could be married to you for this long and not know you? Not understand?"

"Florence . . ."

"I don't agree with everything you've done, Bram," she went on, "but I understand why you've done it. What I need to know now is how much further you intend to go."

He took her hand in both of his.

"There is still so much more I need to learn from him," he said. "The book I'm planning . . . we haven't discussed it, but . . . but—"

"Hush," she said. "This is . . . all so much to take in. All I've known of this man—this Jack the Ripper—is what I've read in the newspapers. Now to discover that my own husband has met him, talked with him . . . I can't say it doesn't frighten me. Do you think he meant what he said?" she asked.

"About what?"

"That he would never hurt me?"

"Oddly," he said, "I do. In his own way I believe his word is important to him."

"Then why didn't you send for me when you knew I would be safe?"

"I . . . had wanted to be *sure* . . ."

"You thought I would try to make you stop," she said, "try to make you go to the police."

"My dear, in an odd way I believe Jack and I have forged a bond, one that we may both benefit from."

She shuddered and hugged herself, rubbing her upper arms.

"Just to hear you say his name that way . . . as if he was a . . . a friend . . ."

"No, not a friend," Stoker said. "I'm not sure how I would describe the relationship we have . . ."

"You may have to describe it to the police at some point, Bram, don't you agree?"

"I suppose so."

She reached out and touched his arm.

"You can't ever believe that by helping the police catch him you would be . . . betraying him, can you?"

"I—I don't know . . ."

"Bram, he's killed so many women."

"I know that, my dear," he said, "yes, I do know that. I assure you, when the time is right I will go to the police."

"Good."

"Meanwhile, perhaps you should return to your mother's in Dublin—"

"My place is with you, Bram," she said, "no matter what madness you involve yourself in. I'm sorry I ever left in the first place. You've had no one to confide all of this to."

"My dear," he said, squeezing her hand, deciding not to tell her of both Harker's and Doyle's involvement. It didn't matter. From this point on she would be his only confidant; he would tell her everything.

Well, almost everything.

"I do have some conditions, however," she warned him.

He sat back. "Name them."

"We cannot stand by and watch this man get away with murder," she said. "After you've spoken to him again we must go to the police."

"All right. Is there another?"

"Yes," she said. "I cannot watch another woman be killed and do nothing. If he strikes again before you have spoken with him, we must go to the police immediately."

"Agreed."

"I do not know if we are doing something foolish, or even stupid," she said, "but when you get past the insanity of it, this becomes quite exciting, doesn't it?"

Chapter Forty-four

On the morning of October 16, Bram Stoker stopped at a peddler's cart for a meat pie before going into the Lyceum Theater for the day. He took it to a bench from which he could see the Thames and there prepared to eat it while reading *The Times*. As he perused the front page he saw the From Hell note printed there in its entirety. Apparently, Mr. George Lusk—whether he felt it was a hoax or not—had taken the note to either the police or the newspapers. The story described Mr. Lusk's horror upon receiving a package containing both the note and the promised kidney.

The story went on to explain that the kidney had been examined and could not be discounted as having belonged to one of the dead women.

After reading the story Stoker laid the newspaper down next to him and proceeded to eat his pie. He was not surprised that reading the news had done nothing to spoil his appetite. In fact, he found the pie very tasty as he ate while watching boats drift down the river.

Over the next few days the newspaper rehashed every aspect of the Ripper murders. They went back and talked about all the past killings, which at the time had not been known as Ripper murders because the murderer had not yet dubbed himself Jack the Ripper. In fact, some of the newspapers still referred to the killings as the Whitechapel murders. Perhaps they felt that by referring to this Ripper by the name of his own choosing they were catering to him. Whatever the newspapers called him, to both Bram and Florence Stoker he had become simply . . . Jack.

As Florence entered her husband's study to bring him a cup of tea, she was surprised at the absolute chaos it reflected.

"My God," she said, setting down the cup on a sticky corner of his desk. "Is your office at the theater like this as well?"

"Hmm?" He looked up from the newspaper report he'd been reading. "I'm sorry, dear?"

"Your office," she said, as if speaking to a deaf person, "at the theater; has it become as bad as this?"

"Oh, worse," he said, "much worse. All the books I've been using to research Vlad are there. I suppose I'll eventually have to bring them back here."

She looked around and, shaking her head, said, "I don't know where you would put them . . . and don't you even think about my kitchen table."

She kissed his brow as he went back to his reading and left him to it.

Later that night Stoker was sitting in the parlor when Florence came up behind him. She put her hands on his shoulders, and he covered her hands with his.

"This book you're going to work on," she said.

"Yes?"

"Where will you write it? Here?"

He hesitated, then said, "I don't know, exactly."

"Will you be able to write it while managing the theater?"

He took one hand from hers and rubbed it across his brow.

"I suppose I'll have to decide that . . . if there even is a theater, when the time comes."

"Why would there not be?"

"Oh, don't pay any attention to me," he said then. "I'm just . . . I'm not really concentrating on theater business these days."

"Because of Jack?"

"Yes."

"And because of this book."

"Yes."

"Do you have a title?"

"No." He thought of the word *Dracula* scrawled across one of his research books in Jack's handwriting. "No, not really."

"Well," she said, "I won't ask you any more questions about it," she said, kissing the top of his head.

"It wouldn't matter," he said, patting her hands before she took them away. "I wouldn't have very much to tell you. Right now I've got more mood than substance, and I haven't even really made any written notes yet. It's all up here." He touched his temple.

She stroked his hair at that temple for a moment and said, "There's so much going on up there, I can almost hear it."

"Then imagine how it must sound to me," he said with a smile.

She kissed him again and said, "Come to bed soon."

"I will. I promise."

She started to leave the parlor when he called her name.

"Yes?"

"Whitby."

"What?"

"You asked where I would write this book," he reminded her. "I'm thinking Whitby. You like it there, don't you?" It was a coast town in Yorkshire where they sometimes summered.

"Why, yes," she said, "we both do."

"Whitby, then," he said. "That'll be the plan."

She smiled, said, "Whitby," and left the room.

Florence Stoker went to the bedroom she shared with her husband and prepared for bed. As she sat brushing her hair she stared fearfully into the mirror, waiting for Jack the Ripper to pop up behind her. She was trying very hard to support her husband, and that meant not letting him know just how much this whole affair frightened her.

She had told her mother nothing of the real reason she had left home in the first place, just that she had come for a visit. When she received the note telling her to come home she had reacted rashly, packed and returned immediately. It was only when Stoker himself pointed out that the note was not in his handwriting that she realized her foolishness. Had she not missed her husband so much . . .

And now to return home and discover who had actually written the note . . . well, a woman of lesser will would have turned and fled immediately. She could not do that, however. If her husband was bound and determined to continue with his . . . quest (for want of a better word), she had to be just as committed to supporting him, no matter how hard it might be.

Chapter Forty-five

Stoker was surprised to find Inspector Swanson waiting for him in front of the Lyceum the next morning.

"Mr. Stoker," the policeman greeted him.

"Inspector. More questions?"

"I am afraid so, and I am equally afraid I would like to ask them at Scotland Yard, if you would not mind accompanying me."

"Am I under arrest?"

"No, sir, you are not. I am requesting that you accompany me to assist in our investigation."

Stoker decided not to test the inspector's resolve in the matter.

"Very well, Inspector. How shall we proceed?"

"I have transportation," Swanson said. He waved

a hand, and a horse-drawn buggy pulled up in front of the theater, driven by a uniformed policeman.

"After you, sir," Swanson said. He climbed into the buggy behind Stoker and shouted, "Drive on."

Upon their arrival at Scotland Yard, located at 4 Whitehall Street, Swanson explained that they were going to the office of the Assistant Commissioner of the CID, Robert Anderson.

"He is my immediate superior," Swanson said, "and would like to speak with you himself."

"I'm honored."

They walked through the CID room, which was bustling with activity, men in and out of uniform, all of whom Stoker assumed were working on the Whitechapel murders. Eventually, Swanson led the way to a door, upon which he knocked.

"Come!" came the call from inside.

Swanson opened the door, allowed Stoker to precede him, entered and closed the door behind them.

"Commissioner Anderson," he said, "this is Bram Stoker."

Anderson, a bearded, elegant-looking man in his fifties, rose from behind his desk and extended his hand.

"Mr. Stoker," he said. "I hope you were treated with the utmost courtesy on your way here."

"Yes, sir," Stoker said. "Inspector Swanson has always treated me respectfully."

The two men shook hands.

"Excellent," Anderson said, "but please don't call

me sir. Uh, why don't you just call me, ah, Commissioner?"

"As you wish," Stoker said.

"Can we get you something, Mr. Stoker? Some tea, perhaps?"

Perhaps because he knew that if he wanted tea the commissioner was going to have to send the inspector to get it, Stoker said yes.

"Inspector?" Anderson said. "Would you get all of us some tea?"

Swanson hesitated a moment, then said, "Yes, sir."

Anderson seemed to want to wait for either the inspector or the tea before getting to the point, so he talked a bit with Stoker about the Lyceum, and how he and his wife had been to the theater many times. Stoker decided to simply let the commissioner dictate the pace of the conversation. He had too much to hide to press the issue at the moment.

Swanson returned with three cups of tea. He handed one each to Stoker and Anderson, then took a seat next to Stoker, holding his cup in his hand. Stoker did the same as the commissioner, setting his cup down on the desk.

"Well, now, Inspector Swanson tells me he thinks you're holding back some information in this Whitechapel fiasco."

Fiasco was not a word Stoker had heard used pertaining to the Jack the Ripper murders.

"Does he?" he asked. "Are we talking about Jack the Ripper?"

Anderson waved his hands, a pained look crossing his face.

"To use that name gives credence to the animal who created it," he said quickly. "Here we continue to refer to him as the Whitechapel killer."

"The newspapers have all adopted the Ripper name."

"Well," Anderson said, patiently, "we have not."

Stoker wondered how Swanson and Anderson perceived him. Certainly the Lyceum Theater catered to the upper crust of London: professional men, lords and ladies, politicians—even the P.M. himself. These were all people who would be treated with great deference by the police. While Swanson and Anderson addressed him politely, did they see him as part of that segment of society? Or was he simply someone who managed a theater, who worked for Henry Irving and was being treated with courtesy rather than respect?

"As you wish," Stoker said. "Has Inspector Swanson told you what it is he believes I'm . . . concealing?"

"Inspector?" Anderson said.

Swanson addressed himself to his superior, rather than to Stoker.

"He knows something, sir. If he doesn't know who this killer is, then I believe he has had contact with him."

"What kind of contact?" Stoker asked. He picked up his teacup, not looking at either man.

Now Swanson looked directly at Stoker.

"We have detected in the correspondence received from the Rip—from this killer, the hand of the journalist. If not a journalist, then certainly a writer."

"I've read all the missives in the newspapers," Stoker said. "It seems to me that the man who wrote them is . . . well, somewhat challenged, shall we say?"

"The inspector does not agree with that assessment, Mr. Stoker," Commissioner Anderson said. The way he said it led Stoker to believe that he, the commissioner, did. "The inspector believes that any grammatical errors have been deliberate. He believes the letters were written by a learned man, possibly a man who is a professional writer."

Stoker stared at Anderson and then asked, "You mean . . . someone like me?"

"The inspector has suggested that you might possibly be the author, yes."

Stoker looked at Swanson. "You believe that I am Jack the Ripper?"

"I never said that," Swanson hurriedly pointed out. "All I said was that I thought you'd had contact with the killer, and might be helping him."

"Why would I help a mad killer?" Stoker asked them both. He was glad the teacup in his hand was not also sitting on a saucer, for the rattling would surely have given away his nervousness.

"Because he might be someone you are acquainted with," Swanson said.

"Are we talking about Henry Irving again?" Stoker asked, contriving to sound exasperated. "I thought you never seriously considered Irving as the killer."

Again Swanson chose to speak to Anderson. "We have witnesses who saw a man fitting Mr. Stoker's description in Whitechapel the night of the two murders. He was with another man who could have been Henry Irving—"

"—dressed as Mr. Hyde," Anderson finished. "Yes, you've told me that."

"The other man could also have been Jack th— the Whitechapel killer, sir."

Stoker looked at Anderson. "The inspector and I have already been through this, Commissioner."

"He seems to feel that since the notes might have been written by a professional such as yourself—"

"I am not the only one who thinks so," Swanson interjected.

"Nevertheless," Commissioner Anderson said, "Mr. Stoker was kind enough to come here at our request to discuss the matter. We are not going to accuse him." Anderson looked at Stoker. "I must, however, ask you, Mr. Stoker, if you have any knowledge of this madman's actions, or if you have in any way assisted him in his gory deeds."

"I have not," Stoker said carefully, "in any way helped Jack the Ripper kill anyone."

"Perhaps not," Swanson said, "but the notes—"

"I did not," Stoker said, "write any letters or notes on behalf of Jack the Ripper."

"The Whitechapel killer," Anderson said.

"Under either name," Stoker added.

Both statements were true, as far as they went.

"Very well, then," the commissioner said. "Thank you for coming, Mr. Stoker. I'm sorry if we've caused you any inconvenience."

"None at all, Commissioner," Stoker said. He rose and set the untouched tea down on the man's desk. "I am happy to assist if I can."

"Commissioner—" Swanson started to protest, but a cold look from his superior cut him off.

"We will discuss it further after Mr. Stoker has left, Inspector."

"Yes, sir."

The man extended his hand and Stoker accepted it, shaking it briefly.

"Again, thank you, sir."

"You're welcome, Commissioner," Stoker said. "I only wish I could have told you something that would have been of help."

That, too, was a statement that was true, as far as it went.

After Stoker left the room both Anderson and Swanson sat down.

"What did you think?" the inspector asked.

"He was very precise in his answers," Anderson said.

"Exactly what I thought."

"All right," Anderson said. "You have permission

to assign someone to watch him. I doubt he's involved, but pursue your present line of inquiry, Inspector."

"Yes, sir," Swanson said. "Thank you, sir."

Part Four

Elementary, My Dear Stoker

Chapter Forty-six

The police did not offer Stoker transportation back to the Lyceum. He realized when he reached the street that this was out of character, considering the deference with which the commissioner had treated him. He suddenly realized—by drawing on his experience of watching so many, many performances on the stage of the Lyceum—that the two men had been putting on a private performance for him. He checked behind himself to see if anyone had come out of the building after him, but there was no one there. That didn't mean, however, that the Metropolitan Police would not now have someone watching him, or actually following him.

He managed to wave down a passing cab and gave the driver the address of the Lyceum. He wasn't concerned with the police because it would not have been difficult for them to predict where he was going and have someone there ahead of him.

During the ride he tried to figure out what this would mean now. With the police suspecting him of having a "relationship" with the Whitechapel killer it was going to be difficult for him to actually continue his meetings with Jack the Ripper. By the time he reached the theater Stoker was angry—angry with the police. They were interfering with his research, which was important to him above all—above the operations of the theater, and above justice.

When the carriage pulled up in front of the theater, Stoker saw Arthur Conan Doyle there waiting for him. He had not seen Conan Doyle since he had come to his house the morning the first Ripper note was printed in the newspapers.

"Bram!" Conan Doyle called out as Stoker stepped down and paid the driver.

"Doyle."

He moved up close to Stoker and asked, "Did you know?"

"Know what?"

"The latest missive, man!" Conan Doyle said. "Had you seen it beforehand?"

Stoker looked around them, up and down the streets, across the way, fruitlessly. He wouldn't have known even if someone were watching them.

"Walk with me," he said.

Conan Doyle started to retort, but Stoker took him by the elbow and moved him along.

"Easy, man!" Conan Doyle said. "You're squeezing the feeling from my arm."

"Sorry," Stoker said, releasing his friend. "Just walk around the corner with me while we talk."

Conan Doyle fell into step with Stoker with some difficulty, since his legs were not as long as his friend's.

"What is happening?"

Briefly, Stoker told Conan Doyle of the questioning he had just endured.

"And you thought they were acting?" Conan Doyle asked when he was finished,

"For my benefit," Stoker said. "The commissioner wanted me to think he was not in agreement with the inspector."

"Who suspects that you have had contact with Jack the Ripper."

"They don't call him that," Stoker said. "They still call him the Whitechapel killer."

"Well, whatever they call him . . . has he been in contact with you again? Did you know about the . . . the kidney?"

Stoker hesitated before answering. It had not been that long since he'd decided that Florence would be his only confidant. He wanted to stay with that decision.

"Doyle," Stoker said, "with the police suspecting me, I think the less you know the better. They might come to you and ask questions you might not want to answer—but will have to."

"I could lie," Doyle said. "I'm a writer, Stoker. I understand your priorities."

"Nevertheless," Stoker said, "I do not wish to put you into a position where you would have to lie."

"So you have heard from him again!"

"We . . . have a certain . . . arrangement."

"Can you contact him?"

"No."

"But if the police suspect you . . . if they decide to watch you from now on . . . it would be his downfall."

They turned the corner onto Burleigh Street.

"He must be caught sooner or later," Stoker said.

"But not until you've gotten what you need from him," Conan Doyle said. "Surely you see that."

"Yes, I do. But I have no way of contacting him. I'm going to have to depend on his guile to protect him, as it has so far."

"I envy you this, Stoker," Conan Doyle said, "this . . . entrée into the madman's mind."

"If, indeed, it can be achieved."

"But surely you must have by now, to some extent, at least."

"Not enough," Stoker said, "not deeply enough. Doyle, I fear two things. One, that I may have only one more chance."

"And the second?"

Stoker looked at his friend, who by this time was huffing and puffing from trying to keep up with his more robust colleague.

"That I shall have no more chances at all."

Chapter Forty-seven

By October 31 Bram Stoker was convinced that his worst fears had been realized. There had not been another murder, and he had not heard from Jack the Ripper again. If that did not change on this night, the entire month of October would have gone by without another incident.

Already the newspapers were wondering if Jack the Ripper was gone. In light of the night of the double murders, the police and all their experts had expected the Whitechapel killer to strike again before the month was out. The compulsion to kill had become too great for him, they said. He would have to kill again, and when he did he would make a mistake and they would catch him.

Well, he hadn't made a mistake yet.

* * *

"What's wrong?" Florence asked Stoker at the breakfast table.

"Nothing," he said. "I'm fine."

"You haven't had a decent meal in days," she said. "You fall asleep on the sofa with your clothes on. You need a haircut, your lovely beard looks . . . well, ratty. What is it, dear?"

He looked across the table at her. "Jack."

"What about him?"

"I think he's gone."

She reached across the table to touch his hand.

"Is that a bad thing?" she asked. "Doesn't that solve everyone's problems?"

"Not mine," he said. "I needed to talk with him one more time, Florence. Just once more!"

"The police are still watching."

"It's their fault," he said bitterly. "They're watching the theater, and I'm sure they're watching the house."

He had said this before, and secretly she had been happy. If they were watching the house, they were both safe.

"How can he get to me if he wants to speak to me?" he asked.

"So you think he's gone away?"

He rubbed his face with both hands. When he took them away his beard stood out on both sides, making it look as if his face had red wings.

"Isn't that sick? If he's gone away the killings will stop and everyone will be happy."

"Don't you think the police would rather catch him?"

"I think they would secretly be happy if he just stopped."

"But . . . if he goes away he might start to kill again somewhere else."

"They would probably prefer that, too."

"Once they stop watching you, and the theater, and our house, maybe he will come back." She hoped he'd *never* come back. She wanted her life—and her husband—back to normal.

"How long will that be?" Stoker asked. "He would have to be a man of infinite patience."

"You don't think he is?"

He held her hand tightly.

"Florence, the times I saw him—the times I was in his presence—there was a . . . an energy about him. Barely contained, even though to the outward eye he might appear calm. I don't think he has the capacity for great patience."

"He's gone a month without killing," she reminded him. "That's patience."

"Or he's gone and, as you said, he might be killing somewhere else."

"What if you started your book, Bram?" she asked. "What if you started to put some of it down on paper?"

He pulled his hand away and stood up, began to pace. As he ran his hands through his hair she thought he was going to tear some of it out.

"I can't," he said. "I'm not ready yet. I need . . ."

"You need . . . Jack?"

He hesitated, then said, "God help me, yes."

"One more time?"

"Yes."

She could not believe what she was going to say next, but maybe it was the only way to get things back to normal.

"Then why are you waiting for him to contact you?"

He stopped pacing and looked at her.

"I don't know where to find him."

"But you know where he's been doing his killing," she said. "What did the newspapers call White-chapel? His 'killing ground'?"

He put his hands on the kitchen table and lowered himself into his chair again.

"Yes," he said, "yes, maybe you're right. With them watching the theater and the house, where else could he find me? It is I who have to do the finding now."

"But . . . aren't the police watching you too? Following you?"

"I'm not certain," he said. "They are professionals, and as such remain undetected."

"Then perhaps you're right," she said, standing up. "Perhaps he is gone and it's all over."

She left the kitchen, left her husband sitting there with his head in his hands. If she knew him as well as she thought she did, he would not let this stop him. His obsession had come much too far for him to stop now. He was a smart man; he would figure out a way. She only hoped that the bond he felt he had with Jack—with a madman—was as strong as he thought it was, and that he would return to her safe and sound—physically, as well as mentally.

Chapter Forty-eight

Stoker tried for several days to figure out a way to get to Whitechapel without the police following him, but he had to admit he was extremely flustered. Thinking that his every move was being watched by the police unnerved him—even more so than when he thought he was being watched by Jack the Ripper. He needed the advice of a much more relaxed and logical mind, and knew where he could get it.

He decided not to go to Conan Doyle's house, or summon the man to the Lyceum. Instead, he waited until he could find Conan Doyle in one of the pubs he frequented to rub elbows with his literary friends. Perhaps the policeman watching him would wait outside the pub and not see who he was talking to.

Naturally, one of the first things Conan Doyle's logical mind did was destroy that theory.

"If you are being followed," Conan Doyle said, "the man is probably here right now, close by."

"I thought, perhaps, he would remain outside."

"And risk your leaving by way of a back door?"

"I hadn't thought of that."

Stoker had to wait until the rest of Conan Doyle's friends/cronies/admirers left before he was able to maneuver him to a table where they could talk alone.

"You *are* flustered, aren't you?"

"Yes," Stoker said, "I am."

"I'm surprised."

"Why?"

Conan Doyle leaned forward.

"Being a confidant of Jack the Ripper's did nothing to unnerve you," he said in a low voice. "Why are the police accomplishing what he could not?"

"I don't know, Doyle," Stoker said. "I only know that I can't seem to think, to reason . . ."

Conan Doyle leaned back.

"You don't look well, old chap."

"I haven't been eating, haven't been sleeping well . . . my personal hygiene has been . . . lacking, I'm afraid."

"Say no more," Conan Doyle said. "I find myself in that same condition when I am . . . engrossed in a story."

"The only difference is," Stoker said, "I haven't written a word yet."

"Tell me why you are concerned about being followed."

Now it was Stoker's turn to lean forward.

"I have not heard from Jack in some time. I'm afraid the police might be keeping him away."

"You think they've caught him?"

Stoker blinked. That had not occurred to him.

"If they had, I think we would have read about it in the newspapers, don't you? With the city up in arms, they certainly would have announced his capture."

"I agree," Conan Doyle said. "It was just a thought. So you feel he can't get near you because of the police?"

"Yes."

"And you want to go and find him."

"Exactly." Stoker was impressed.

"Just a logical assumption," Conan Doyle said.

"I want to go to Whitechapel without being followed," Stoker said. "How can I accomplish that?"

"You buy us two more pints," Conan Doyle said, "while I ponder the question."

"All right."

Stoker got up and walked to the bar to order. While he waited he looked around the pub, wondering which of the men drinking there was a policeman. He finally gave up because they all looked like policemen, and they all did not.

"Here ya go," the barman said, setting two fresh pints on the bar.

"Thank you."

Stoker carried them back to the table, set one down in front of Conan Doyle and reseated himself with the other.

"Anything?"

"Perhaps," Conan Doyle said. "Let me ask you a few questions about the theater, and your route to and from it."

"Fine."

Stoker answered all Conan Doyle's questions, making his replies as forthcoming as he could.

"Hmm," Conan Doyle finally said. "It seems that using the Burleigh Street exit is not an option. They would probably have a man watching that door as well."

"So what does that leave us?"

"I do have one idea."

"I am listening."

Conan Doyle spoke for a couple of minutes while Stoker listened. When the physician was done Stoker shook his head. "That's not an idea, that's a solution, and a brilliant one. Why didn't I think of it?"

"I don't know," Conan Doyle said. "It's quite elementary, my dear Stoker."

Chapter Forty-nine

Stoker went to the Lyceum on November 1 with Conan Doyle's plan firmly in mind. He would, however, need to collect a few things from the theater so he could put the plan—the very *elementary* plan, as his friend had pointed out—into motion the next day.

He was down in the wardrobe room in the basement when Henry Irving entered and stood just inside the doorway.

"Bram," Irving said, "I've been looking for you."

"I've been right here, chief," Stoker said, not looking up from what he was doing.

"No," Irving said, "I mean, I've been looking for you for days. I went to your office, but it's a bloody mess in there."

"I know," Stoker said. "I've been, uh, doing some research, and . . ."

The rest of what he said was muffled because he leaned down to pull something from a trunk.

"Bram," Irving said, "can we talk?"

"Of course, guv," Stoker said, "I'm just a little busy—"

"Bram!" Irving's voice was sharp and brought Stoker around to look at him. "What has been going on? Your office is in ruins, no one has seen you for days, and look at you. You look . . . a mess."

Stoker used one hand to smooth down his hair and the other to brush his beard.

"Now what's going on?" Irving asked, with great concern for his friend—and the Lyceum as well. "My theater manager is not managing so well these days."

"Henry," Stoker said, "I just need some time. I'm involved in something that needs my attention—"

"More than the Lyceum does?" Irving asked. "We need to get *Macbeth* up and running, Bram."

"It's not actually my fault that it's taken this long, Henry."

Chagrined, Irving looked away for a moment before again making eye contact.

"I realized my . . . behavior has endangered our season as much as anything else. I'm trying to make up for that. In fact, I have a meeting with Prime Minister Primrose tomorrow to discuss this ban on *Dr. Jekyll and Mr. Hyde.*"

Irving came farther into the room and stood a few

feet from Stoker, who was holding several items in his hand—a hat, a ratty wig . . .

"Bram, you helped me when I most needed you. I admit I was falling into an abyss . . . I was . . . *enthralled* with the character of Mr. Hyde, but you pulled me out. You showed me the danger in what I was doing. What are *you* doing, Bram . . . and is it dangerous? Can I help?"

"Maybe you can, Henry," Stoker said. "There are a few items I need and I can't find them in here. Perhaps in your wardrobe . . ."

"Come upstairs," Irving said. "You can have anything you want, but you must tell me what's going on, and how long it will be before you can get back to work . . . and we can all return to normal."

"Return to normal," Stoker repeated. "I don't really know if that's possible, Henry." He dropped what he was holding and brushed off his hands. "I'll try to explain. Maybe you, of all people, will understand."

Stoker explained as much as he could to Irving—his research, his need to be able to move around without the police watching him. However, he could not bring himself to tell his friend about his special relationship with Jack the Ripper. Rather, he simply let Irving believe that he was as obsessed with the Ripper as Irving had been with Mr. Hyde—perhaps even more so.

"I understand obsession," Irving said. "I of all people certainly understand that. And I understand the . . . the artistic strain you must be under."

Robert J. Randisi

"Can you help me?"

"I would like to help you the way you helped me," Irving said. "I'd like to persuade you to give this up."

"I can't, Henry," Stoker said. "Not just now. I have only a few more things to do before I can start my book."

"And Florence? She understands all this?"

"Yes."

"And supports it?"

"Oh, she's not happy with it," Stoker said. "Henry . . . I need to do this. That is what she understands."

"Very well. It took finding a dead woman to bring me back to reality. I do not want the same for you."

Irving had been sitting at his dressing table. Now he stood and walked to his wardrobe. He removed a few items, turned and said, "Take these." Then he walked back to the dressing table and removed a few things. "And take these. You really shouldn't need anything else—except, perhaps, some advice on . . . how to walk."

They remained in Irving's dressing room for a good half hour, with Irving as the teacher and Stoker the student.

"I think I've got it," Stoker said.

"To an extent," Irving said doubtfully. "You don't have to go on stage in front of hundreds of people, though. You simply have to fool one or two people, am I right?"

"I hope so."

"You can simply roll these up," Irving said, demonstrating, "with these inside. There. You have a small bundle."

Stoker accepted the bundle and said, "I truly appreciate this, Henry."

"Do what you have to do, Bram," Irving said. "Lord knows I've always done so. Just . . . be sure to come back, eh? We have a lot of work to do."

"I'll be back, chief," Stoker said. "I promise."

"I hope so," Irving said, but Stoker was already rushing out the door.

Chapter Fifty

The next morning Bram Stoker's resolve to make Florence his total confidant took a fatal blow.

"What is that?" she asked, seeing the bundle he had under his arm as he readied himself to leave.

"Just some things Henry wanted me to bring to him," Stoker lied. While going out in search of Jack was technically her idea, he decided to keep it from her until he had either failed or succeeded.

Whether she believed him or not she did not question him again.

The ferry was never crowded when Stoker took it each morning, and in his head he had already chosen the corner he would use to make his transformation.

Despite the fact that he was a large man, the clothing he had borrowed from Henry Irving fit right over what he was wearing. The fabric was very thin, easily donned and removed. It was made for the quick changes necessary on stage.

The night before he had finally relented and agreed to allow Florence to cut both his hair and beard.

"Why this sudden interest in your grooming?" she'd asked suspiciously.

"I have always taken great pride in my appearance."

"Yes, but not recently," she said. "Does this signal some sort of return to normalcy?" Her tone became hopeful at that point.

"Perhaps," he said. "Or perhaps I just looked in the mirror for the first time in a long while."

She heaved a great sigh and began to snip away.

"Cut it short, so I won't have to deal with it for a while," he suggested.

When he came down for breakfast the next morning he had been wearing a suit and tie—he'd forgone ties for the longest time, not having the patience to tie them—and looked impeccable. In fact, he thought he looked more normal than he had in some time—except for the bundle beneath his arm.

Now, as he took out the dye Irving had given him and began to apply it to his newly shorn beard, he realized Florence had not believed anything he'd said to her that morning, or the evening before. She had simply decided to leave him alone in the hope that he would eventually come back to his senses. Well, if she could see him now, crudely coloring his beard black because he had no proper mirror to use, settling instead for the glass window he was seated next to, she would probably think that day was still far off.

When he was done his beard might not have been completely black, but at least it was no longer red. He tucked the tube of coloring solution into the pocket of Irving's great coat and withdrew from the other pocket a cloth cap, which he pulled onto his head, entirely covering his red hair. From a distance he would now be—he hoped—unrecognizable when he left the ferry.

He looked around to see if he'd successfully completed the transformation without notice. Most of his fellow passengers were either gazing out at the water, reading the morning newspaper or engrossed in whatever literature their occupations dictated they read. Whatever they were doing, they were not paying any attention to him.

Conan Doyle's plan for him to alter his appearance while on the ferry was predicated upon not having a policeman on the ferry with him.

"It is my belief," his friend had said, "that they will have a man on either side of the Thames watching for you. To actually have a man board the ferry with you would risk your seeing him."

"I've seen no one," Stoker said. "For all I know

this is all for naught and they are not even having me watched."

"Nevertheless," Conan Doyle said, "it is better to err on the side of caution."

"Is that something Sherlock Holmes says in your stories?"

Conan Doyle waved a hand dismissively and said, "It's entirely too banal for Holmes. It is more along the lines of something a London physician would say."

As the ferry docked Stoker thought about erring on the side of caution and considered it a good idea. He decided to disembark in the middle of a group of people rather then get off first, as he always did, or last on this day. He stuck his hands deep into the pockets of Irving's coat, kept his head down and kept pace with others. It was a cool morning, so the coat did not appear out of place at all. He tried not to look around for a policeman, contriving rather to appear as bored as the others. His instinct was to hunch his shoulders, but he made a concerted effort not to do so.

As he got farther from the ferry and the people began to scatter he started to feel safe. He didn't turn, didn't look behind him. Instead he kept going, crossing the street, turning down an alley. He thought about removing his disguise there but decided against it. First, he would find a cab for hire and have it take him to Whitechapel. Even when he arrived there, it would probably make more sense to remain in his disguise. He'd fit in much better. Once he removed Irving's coat the quality of his clothes would make him stand out.

The deciding factor finally came when he waved down a cab. The driver took one look at him and asked, "Can you pay?"

Chapter Fifty-one

It was odd how much more welcoming the streets of Whitechapel felt to him dressed the way he was. Where he would have been stared at standing in front of the Lyceum Theater dressed this way, here in Whitechapel his look was normal. This was the only time he'd ever gone to London's East End when he was able to move about freely. However, he quickly learned that this was not what he needed.

Being an accepted member of the East End community meant he didn't speak to anyone, and nobody spoke to him. These people went about their own business and didn't have time for idle chatter. Once or twice he tripped as he walked down streets where the cobblestones were broken and jagged. Nobody was going to come around and fix them, either. The blood from the Ripper's victims stayed in the grooves between the stone until the rain came and washed it away. The garbage stayed where it was until dogs or rats came to eat it.

For just for a moment Stoker thought that maybe Jack the Ripper was not killing women who lived here, worked here, but was saving them.

Late in the day he realized he was dressed all wrong for what he was trying to accomplish. If Jack was going to hear that Stoker was looking for him, he was going to have to attract attention, like before, and not blend in. He finally decided to pick an alley—there were certainly enough of them—and divest himself of his disguise.

He removed the hat and Irving's coat; the only thing he couldn't change was the color of his beard. He'd need a bath to do that, and there wasn't one to be had here. He knew his black beard would look odd with his red hair, but there was nothing he could do. He didn't want to carry the coat around with him, so he decided to take a chance and hide it. He rolled it up with the hat in the pocket and deposited it behind some crates. He hoped it would still be there when he returned. If not, he would have to find a way to make it up to his friend.

When he stepped from the alley he immediately caught the attention of a man and woman walking by, both of whom pointed to him and made mention of the "toff" who was down here "slumming."

Yes, this would be much better.

* * *

Walking around Whitechapel now was an entirely different matter. He was now the curiosity on the street, dressed as he was in his dark suit and tie. He considered removing the tie but thought that would look even more odd. He wanted to ask questions, but people were unwilling to talk to him. He thought about going back to the Bloody Bucket to talk to the bartender there, but the last time he'd been there he and Harker had almost been killed by a band of villains. The bartender had most certainly been in on that.

As it started to get darker he realized what a fool's errand this had been. If Jack the Ripper was gone, then he was gone. Wandering aimlessly around Whitechapel trying to find him would not bring him back.

As it grew later still he wished he'd kept Irving's coat; it was starting to get cool. He stepped into a doorway, arms folded across his chest. While standing there two women walked by, and when they saw him they gasped and started to run. It took him a moment to realize that they were running from him. He turned and caught a look at himself in the glass of the door behind him. The odd dichotomy of the red hair and black beard was the least of it. He looked gaunt, and his eyes appeared red rimmed. He'd frightened those poor women with his bizarre appearance, and they had run from him as if he were Jack the Ripper himself.

The shock of this struck him like a bucket of cold

water. What was he doing here, haunting the alleys of Whitechapel like a madman—*searching* for another madman? Here then was *his* dead body, the thing that yanked him back to his senses. If the Ripper was gone, so be it. What a fool he had been to think that he could forge a bond with someone like that. The man could have turned on him and killed him at any time. The realization of *that* robbed his legs of strength and he almost crumpled to the ground.

He quit the doorway. Suddenly anxious to leave Whitechapel, he was disoriented. He didn't know where the alley was in which he'd secreted Irving's coat, and he didn't know which way Whitechapel Road was. He knew only one thing.

He needed to get home.

He finally managed to locate Whitechapel Road, his landmark. From there he flagged down a cab and told the driver to take him where he could catch the ferry back across the Thames. He'd have to come back for Irving's coat in the daylight.

When he reached the Thames ferry he wasn't certain whether a policeman who might or might not be watching for him would be able to recognize him, and he didn't care. He just wanted to get on the ferry and get home to Florence. Maybe he'd hear from Jack the Ripper again and maybe he would not, but he had to stop all this irrational behavior before it got completely out of hand—before he lost his mind!

Once on the ferry the pounding of his heart began to slow. He stared across at the lights on the other side of the river. His heartbeat had almost returned to normal when a voice from behind spoke directly into his ear—so close that he could feel the heat of the speaker's breath.

"Looking for me is a breach of our agreement, Bram."

Chapter Fifty-two

The last hours of Mary Jane Kelly's life were not the most pleasant—but then, there were not many parts of her twenty-five years that were.

She resided in Miller's Court off Dorset Street, at 12 McCarthy Rents. There were at least two other women in the McCarthy rents who walked the streets to make their living. Mary Jane had been living with a man named Joseph Barnett until two weeks earlier, when he moved out after a fight over her career of choice. Now five weeks in arrears on her rent, Mary Jane spent those last hours trying to make the five times four shillings and sixpence she needed.

That she became the Ripper's final victim was quite by chance.

*　*　*

Jack watched Mary Jane Kelly as she entered the Ten Bells Pub on the corner of Church and Commercial streets, just around the corner and down the street from her rooms. He'd not been looking for a victim this night, but he was so immediately offended by her that he could not resist. She was young—the youngest yet—and as such could probably have chosen a different path for herself. That she had not, and had taken what he considered the easy way out—what easier way for a woman to make her living than on her knees in an alley, or her back in a dirty room?—incensed him.

In truth, Jack *had* decided that he was done with the killing, until speaking with Bram Stoker. Catherine Eddowes was not intended to be the last. In fact, Jack had never known who would be last. He went out and found his next victim when the urge, the hunger, came over him. The urge was to kill, the hunger was for blood. For some reason, however, he had managed to go through the entire month of October without feeling either. And he did have another life—his real life—to get back to. This . . . spree he'd been on had never been intended to go on for very long. In the beginning he was just . . . testing himself, trying to find out how far, how deep the urge and the hunger went. There was a time—a frightening time, in the dark dead of one night—when he thought they would be endless. That changed, however, after the Night of the Two Victims. He might not have thought it possible, but later, upon reflection, he wondered if he had overdone it—overdosed, perhaps. Suddenly the endless had an end; the emptiness was filled.

Or was it?

There had still been one thing he'd wanted to do, and that was speak with Bram Stoker again. Stoker understood him. Oh, he had no illusions that the writer approved of what he'd been doing, but he *understood,* of that he had no doubt.

But when he tried to see Stoker at the Lyceum again he noticed the theater was being watched. He went to his house, but there he also found a policeman lurking. It would have been a relatively simple thing to kill the man and go in anyway, but he had no stomach for that. The policeman had done nothing to him, did not deserve to die. The only men he had killed had been those thieves who had attacked Stoker and his friend. They deserved to die. Jack did not kill innocent people or those who didn't satisfy his hungers.

Also, he decided not to go into Stoker's home because his wife had returned. He was pleased that his note had worked, had brought his friend's wife back to him. He would abide by his word and never threaten Florence Stoker. Neither did he wish to frighten her, and entering her house would have done just that.

So Jack had to follow Stoker—follow behind the men who were already following him, watching him. Stoker's clumsy attempt at a disguise had not fooled Jack the way it had the policemen. Jack had been behind him all the way to Whitechapel. Once he realized Stoker was simply wandering aimlessly he decided to wait until the man had exhausted himself. There was still a policeman watching the ferry, but that didn't matter. No one knew what Jack looked like, and he did not board the ferry until after dark.

Then he just waited.

"Why were you looking for me?" Jack asked.

Stoker's first instinct had been to turn around, but he quelled it. He realized the fear he had not been feeling for weeks was back, the fear that Jack might kill him. Had the fear returned because his sanity had also?

"Stoker?"

"I . . . I wanted to talk to you, one last time, and I thought the police might be watching me."

"You thought?"

"I-I couldn't be sure."

"Be sure," Jack said. "They had been watching you, your every move, until you lost them today with your . . . um, disguise."

Stoker's hand went to his beard.

"You saw that?"

"Indeed. Here, you might want this back." Two hands came over his left shoulder and deposited a bundle into his lap. It was Henry Irving's coat.

"You knew I was looking for you?"

"I've been behind you every minute," Jack said.

"Until after dark, anyway, when I came here to wait for you."

"But . . . why didn't you approach me earlier?"

"I was waiting for you to come to your senses," Jack said. "Have you?"

"I believe so."

"So have I."

"What does that mean?"

"That I'm finished."

"No more killing?" Stoker asked. "Just like that?"

"Just like that."

Stoker didn't know what to say.

"What about your hunger?" Jack asked. "Your hunger for knowledge? Is it gone?"

"My hunger . . ."

"You wanted to know about me, and about man's dark side. Don't you have any questions for me?"

Stoker thought a moment and then surprised himself by saying, "No."

"You searched for me all day and have no question now?"

"I . . . suppose . . ."

"Do you know why?"

Helplessly, Stoker said, "No."

"Because you have all your answers," Jack said. "You just don't know it."

"I . . . I don't think—"

"You need to go away and think about it. It's all there, inside your head. You just need to let it come out."

"And what about you?" Stoker asked. "The newspapers are filled with . . . with Jack the Ripper. The populace is up in arms, vigilante groups are forming, the police are baffled, the Crown is considering getting involved . . . and you can just stop?"

Jack thought a moment, then put his hand on Stoker's shoulder, squeezed and said, "Well, when you put it that way . . ."

"I turned and he was gone!" Stoker said to Florence. He stared down at the water in the sink, stained black by the coloring he'd washed out of his beard.

"Thank God," she said. "Let's hope that he's gone forever."

"But—but that's just it," Stoker said, turning to face her. He accepted the towel she thrust into his hands. "Don't you see?"

"See what, dear?"

"He'd already decided to stop," he said, "to quit. I may have talked him out of it!"

"Nonsense," she said. "No one made him start, and no one can make him stop. You can't take any responsibility for what he's done."

"I know that," he said. "But what if I'm responsible for what he does from now on?"

Chapter Fifty-three

Mary Jane Kelly had no idea that she had been sentenced to death twice. Sentenced, reprieved, then sentenced again. Jack changed his mind, then changed it again. Finally, even though he had only chanced upon Mary Jane, the hunger arrived and, once there, could not be ignored or denied.

She left the Ten Bells with a blotchy-faced man and they walked along Commercial Street arm in arm, unaware that she was being followed. They turned into Dorset Street, and then into Miller's Court. She took the man to her room, where they remained for several hours. At times, singing could be heard coming from room twelve.

* * *

Robert J. Randisi

As Jack stalked her he had no pity for her. The one he felt sorry for was Bram Stoker. The writer was going to feel tremendous guilt when he read about Mary Jane's demise. There was no avoiding it. And well he should, for Jack *was* done—Mary Jane *would* have lived—if Stoker had not, quite unwittingly, talked Jack out of it.

Mary Jane's time spent with the blotchy-faced man had not earned her enough for her rent, so after he left she came back out and started walking back up Commercial Street, toward the Ten Bells.

That was where she met Jack.

Jack had decided to do this one indoors, where he could work at his leisure, with no danger of being discovered. After all, the woman was a known prostitute, taking a man to her room.

Who was going to care?

This was his masterpiece. He realized now that he never should have doubted this one. He carved her from face to pubes after cutting her throat. He sliced her face and arms and then opened her and emptied her out. The blood saturated her bed as he worked. He placed her kidneys and one breast beneath her head; the other breast he positioned by the right foot. He never had a doubt where he was going to place her parts because he could see it in his head, as if he was working from a painting. He placed her liver between her feet, her intestines next to her on the left side and her spleen on her right—

326

and then he exchanged them and stepped back. Yes, this was right. Perfect.

He skinned her then, just certain parts, like her thighs, one buttock. He exposed her right down to the bone. As she was still young her skin was smooth and soft. The smell of her blood permeated the room, made him so dizzy at times that he had to stop and then start again. The sensation was almost orgasmic, making his hands tremble. In the end he left her left lung intact but removed her heart and took it with him.

Before leaving, however, he made one last cut, this on one of her thumbs, and then held the wound to his mouth. . . .

He wondered if he should send Stoker a thank-you note but thought better of it. The guilt was going to be bad enough. He liked Stoker, and hoped that someday he'd be able to get over it. If he did, he knew Bram Stoker was going to come out of this experience with a brilliant book. A book which, by all rights, he should dedicate to "My friend, Jack the Ripper."

No, it should say, "To my friend, Jack the Ripper, for showing me the tangled and dark side of man."

Chapter Fifty-four

Jack the Ripper's prediction of Bram Stoker's reaction when he read of Mary Jane Kelly's murder was quite accurate. The surge of guilt that coursed through his body at the breakfast table was like a physical blow.

"Bram, darling . . ." Florence said, trying to appease him, but he would have none of it.

"My fault," he said, slamming down the newspaper, "my bloody fault, damn it!"

"Bram," she said, "he did what he was going to do. You couldn't have talked him into, or out of, any—"

"You don't understand!" he said, leaping to his feet. "It's not only that. I've been so caught up in myself, in my book . . . if I had gone to the police

329

in the beginning they might have caught him by now. I might have saved this woman—or the others."

"Now you're the savior of all women of London?" she asked him. "When did you assume that mantle?"

"Not all women, Florence." He sat down, suddenly very weary. "Perhaps this one, though. Perhaps . . ."

She reached across the table and stroked his cheek.

"It's over, Bram. It's done."

"Is it? How do we know he won't do it again, and again? I must go to the police."

"And tell them what?" she asked. "That you might have helped catch him if you had only spoken up sooner? Well, you didn't, and I won't have you turning yourself in now to be arrested for . . . for . . . oh, for whatever they would charge you with."

"Obstruction, I suppose."

"I don't care!"

Her tone was suddenly vehement, and he looked at her in shock.

"I won't trade you for the lives of those . . . those East End women. I won't, I tell you." Her hand closed over his sleeve and held it tightly. "Promise me you won't go to the police. Promise!"

"All right," he said, taking her hand in both of his, "all right, dear. I promise."

But as he said the words he did not know if it was

a promise he would be able to keep if the Ripper struck again.

But he never heard from Jack the Ripper again, and neither did anyone else. Oh, there were other murders in London, some of which the newspapers might have used to sell papers or a vigilante group might have used to enhance their reputation.

A whore named Rose Mylett—whose real name was Lizzie Davis—was killed on December 20, but the police quickly determined that this was not the work of Jack the Ripper.

Another prostitute, Alice McKenzie, was murdered on July 17, 1889, but as her wounds were neither as severe nor as intimate, this was not deemed a "Ripper" murder.

On September 10, 1889, the torso of an unknown woman was discovered on Pinchin Street, in Whitechapel, but again it was not the work of Jack the Ripper.

And the final murder anyone attempted to attribute to Jack came on February 13, 1891. An extensive investigation was launched into this one, but in the end it too was attributed to some killer other than Jack the Ripper.

In December 1888 the Lyceum Theater launched its run of *Macbeth,* even though in the absence of Jack the Ripper it might have once again taken up *Dr. Jekyll and Mr. Hyde.* It was Henry Irving's decision, however, to forgo any further performances of that play. Immersing himself once again in the character of Henry Hyde was a pleasure he decided to postpone—perhaps indefinitely.

On opening night among the dignitaries present were Inspector Donald Swanson and his wife. Stoker—knowing in advance that the inspector and his wife had purchased tickets—made certain the Swansons received an invitation to dine in the Beefsteak Room after the performance. Mrs. Swanson seemed quite beside herself with pleasure at dinner, while the inspector seemed to spend much of his time glowering across the table at Stoker.

It was not until after dinner that Stoker found himself accosted by the inspector.

"A word, Mr. Stoker?" the man asked, abruptly interrupting a conversation Stoker was having with Arthur Conan Doyle and Oscar Wilde.

"Of course, Inspector."

When neither Conan Doyle nor Wilde made an attempt to leave the inspector said, "In private?"

Conan Doyle and Wilde exchanged a glance, then each exchanged a nod with Stoker before wandering off to leave the two men alone.

"I hope your wife enjoyed the performance? And dinner?" Stoker asked.

"Yes," the inspector said, "she has enjoyed the entire evening immensely." He looked over to where his wife was deeply involved in an animated discussion with Lady Macbeth herself, Ellen Terry.

"And you, Inspector? You have not enjoyed the evening?"

"I enjoyed the play very much," Swanson said, "but I found it difficult to eat my dinner while sitting at the table with a man who has aided and abetted a madman guilty of killing innocent women in London."

"By that remark I assume you still believe that I had something to do with Jack the Ripper's—what have the newspapers been calling it—'reign of terror.' "

"Indeed, it has been a reign of terror, and I don't only think you helped him, I know you did."

Stoker's heart was beating wildly. He hoped his condition was not reflected in either his appearance or his voice.

"And what is it you believe I did, Inspector? Did I hold the women down while he flayed them?"

Swanson assumed a look of such disgust that Stoker thought the man was about to spit.

"Oh, you didn't get blood on *your* hands, sir," the policeman said, "but I believe that, had you come forward at some point during this investigation, you might have saved one, two or possibly three women."

"And you, Inspector, might have saved them if you had captured the murderer."

"Oh, we are both culpable, sir," Swanson agreed, "that is certainly true, but with one proviso—I, and the men under my command, at least *tried* to catch him."

"Inspector—"

Robert J. Randisi

Swanson cut him off by poking him in the chest with a stiffened forefinger.

"The Whitechapel killer will return, sir," Swanson said, "and if he contacts you when he does I pity you if you do not contact me immediately."

"And if I do not?"

"Then you had better hope he came back to kill *you.*"

After Swanson stormed away Stoker felt the sweat break out on his brow.

"Well," Oscar Wilde said, appearing at his elbow, "now the evening gets interesting, huh?"

Stoker turned and looked at his friend.

"Bram, you're pale," Wilde said, suddenly concerned for his friend. "Are you feeling all right?"

"I'm all right, Oscar," Stoker assured him.

"Was it something that disagreeable policeman said?"

"Truly, my friend," Stoker said, "I'm fine. Did you enjoy the evening?"

"Up to now? Yes, very much."

"Good, good. It was a delight, as always to see you."

Oscar Wilde might have played the fool on occasion, but he was not one. He knew something was bothering his friend, might even have had an inkling as to what it was, but he did not pursue the matter.

"Very well," he said, shaking Stoker's hand. "Call on me if you need to talk."

"I will," Stoker assured his friend. "Thank you, Oscar."

Wilde went off to bid good night to Henry Irving, Ellen Terry and the others, leaving Stoker alone, standing on shaky legs. Suddenly he felt as if he would faint, when strong hands took hold of his arms from behind.

"Out in the hall," Arthur Conan Doyle said.

"Yes," Stoker said weakly.

Conan Doyle steered Stoker through a door and into a hall where he could stand with his back to the wall.

"Do you require a chair?" the physician asked.

"No."

"You're pale and perspiring. Are you ill?" Conan Doyle began to take Stoker's pulse.

"Ill, yes, Doyle," Stoker said, "but not physically."

Conan Doyle stood back and regarded Stoker critically.

"Was it something that passed between you and the inspector that has caused this condition?"

"Oh, indeed, Doyle, indeed," Stoker said.

"Jack the Ripper?"

Stoker nodded.

"I believe I can guess what it was," Conan Doyle said. "The inspector holds you responsible, does he not? For some of the Ripper's actions?"

"Yes," Stoker said, "and he is not the only one."

"Bram," Conan Doyle asked, "was there ever a time when you might have overpowered the Ripper and captured him?"

"I don't—"

"Answer me."

"No, there was not."

"Was there a time when you might have run and fetched the inspector in time to capture him?"

"No, I don't think so."

"Are you even certain—one hundred percent certain!—that the man you have spoken to on—what?—several occasions *was* indeed Jack the Ripper?"

"Well, I—"

"Without the shadow of a doubt, sir?"

Stoker hesitated, then said, "No."

"You've done nothing but have conversations with a man on several occasions who claimed to be Jack the Ripper."

"But the notes—"

"Don't be so hard on yourself, Bram," Conan Doyle said. "This is medical advice, now. Jack the Ripper is most likely gone, never to return."

"How—how can you be sure of that?"

"Look at the murders, my friend," Conan Doyle said. "In the parlance of you theatrical people, doesn't his last performance smack of a *finale?*"

Stoker regained some strength in his legs and took back his weight from the wall.

"Possibly," he admitted.

"Not possibly, Stoker," Conan Doyle said, "Positively."

Epilogue
Whitby, Yorkshire
Summer 1890

1

Two years of guilt was enough for any man.

All that time, after the grizzly murders, Jack had not been heard from again—not by the police, the press or—thank God—Bram Stoker.

He had been unable to begin work on his book because of the guilt he felt. He never told the police about his relationship with Jack. With the man disappearing and the killings stopping, there seemed no need. The veil of fear the Ripper murders had cast over the city—specifically the East End—slowly began to lift. Oh, now and then there'd be a murder that someone would try to blame the Ripper for, but they'd never stick.

Stoker, however, did not deal well with the guilt of Mary Jane Kelly's death. After the news of her murder he felt certain he had talked Jack into killing her. That was something he found difficult to live with.

He stopped thinking about the book and in fact did not write anything at all for six months. He did, however, manage to get his work at the Lyceum back on track, and the production of *Macbeth* was a huge success. But the special book that had been so important to him, important enough for him to risk everything, remained dormant . . . until Whitby.

They had decided a three-week holiday was greatly needed, and after an eight-hour train ride Stoker and Florence secured a suite at 6 Royal Crescent, a hotel situated on the West Cliff of Whitby. From their balcony they had a view of the sea. Stoker was immediately taken with Whitby. While Florence seemed content to sit in their room, or on the balcony, Stoker immediately began walking around the small seaside resort, which had once been a simple fishing village.

A casualty of the Jack the Ripper experience seemed to have been Stoker's relationship with his wife. It had been a gradual process during all the months since the killings. Hoping the change of scenery would bring back their happiness, Stoker tried while Florence made little effort.

And so Stoker found himself wandering Whitby alone. There were many days when he climbed the 199 steps leading up the cliff to St. Mary's Church. The steps, though they numbered one less than 200, were not a steep climb. Indeed, he would later write that "the slope was so gentle a horse could easily walk up and down them."

At the top of the steps Stoker spent time with some of the older locals, who gathered in the churchyard, recalling the old days of fishing, telling stories of drownings and shipwrecks. Stoker began to take notes, especially on the fishermen's accents. One day, while strolling the graveyard, writing down names that fascinated him that he might use later in a novel, he realized something, making him stop cold in his tracks.

That night, two years before, in the theater, with Jack the Ripper on the stage, the killer had obviously dropped his guard, but when he spoke he used words Stoker had not heard before, in an accent strange to him. Now he recognized that accent as being from Yorkshire, and he'd heard the fisherman use the word *tha* when he could have said *you.* He still didn't know what *gormless* meant, however. And so he found someone to ask.

An old fisherman named Barnaby accepted Stoker's invitation to the small pub called the Wayfarer. Over a pint he asked the man what the word *gormless* meant.

"Where'd ya hear that word, now?" the older man asked. He must have been seventy, and his once clear blue eyes were watery, with a white discharge coming from the corners. Stoker wondered why the man didn't wipe it away, then realized it probably did no good. He wondered how well the man could truly see.

"I just heard it, wondered what it was."

"Aye, well, as long as it warn't someone sayin' it to you."

"Why is that?"

"They'd be callin' ya stupid," Barnaby said. " 'At's what the word means hereabouts . . . stupid."

"And it's only used around here?"

"Not jest Whitby," the man said, "but aye, it's pure Yorkshire."

Good God, Stoker thought, Jack the Ripper was from Yorkshire.

"Please," Florence said later, when he told her what he had found out, "this is not something I want to start again, Bram. No more Jack the Ripper."

"But . . . but don't you see, dear?" Stoker asked. "He was from here."

"If he is from here, then I want to leave," she said forcefully.

"Well," Stoker said, "not from here, not Whitby. I mean, from somewhere in Yorkshire."

"And how many villages are there in Yorkshire, Bram?" she demanded.

"I don't know," he said, "maybe hund—"

"And do you intend to search them all?"

"No, of course not."

"Are you thinking again that it should fall to you

to catch the Ripper, even two years after the fact?"

"No," he said, "I don't want to catch him—"

"Then stop it," she snapped. "Stop talking about it. I am going to sit on the balcony and watch the sea."

"But Florence, the village is lovely. Come and have something—"

"I will be on the balcony," she said again. "And it is there I will dine this evening."

"Oh, very well," he said, and left her there.

He spent the remainder of that day walking through the beautiful Whitby Abbey, built during the twelfth century. He walked along the cliffs, looking down over the village and the beaches. He wished Florence were there to share it with him and wondered if he could find anything to lure her out of her room.

Several days later he discovered that a travelling theatrical group was putting on a production of *The Marriage of Figaro.* Armed with this news, he was able to convince Florence to leave the room and attend a performance. Once outside she discovered that there were also dances and concerts and teas available at a nearby spa. They attended several of these over the course of a week. While Florence remained distant when they were alone in their room together, at least they were able to enjoy a few carefree moments.

One of the things he enjoyed alone, however, was

the Whitby Library. And there, among the 3000 tomes, he finally found the impetus to begin putting words to paper.

He found Dracula.

2

From the shelves of the Whitby Library, Bram Stoker pulled a book with the call number 0.1097, which he later documented in his notes. This was a book entitled *An Account of the Principalities of Wallachia and Moldavia* by William Wilkinson. It was only after he had the book in his hands that he realized it was a different edition of a book he had read two years earlier to research Vlad the Impaler. Now that he had it in his hands again he decided to reacquaint himself with it.

He spent hours pouring over the book and, late in the day, while reading about the Carpathians, came upon a section dealing with the word *Dracula*. His earlier reading had indicated that this was part of Vlad's name, and meant *Son of the Dragon*. In this edition, however, it explained that: "Dracula in the Wallachian language means Devil." It also informed him that Wallachians became accustomed to giving this as a surname to any man who exhibited an unusual degree of cruelty and cunning. This, of course, described Vlad perfectly.

And it was at this moment that Stoker opened his notebook and made the first notes for the novel he would later call *Dracula*.

Although he originally wrote down the title *The Dead Un-dead* for this book, it nevertheless became *Dracula*. He had no way of knowing that the pages of notes he scribbled that day were just the beginning for him, of many days and nights of immersing himself in the world of his un-dead antagonist Dracula—who was, certainly to his mind, part Vlad the Impaler, part Devil and part Jack the Ripper.

He returned to the suite exhausted, and kept the notes hidden from Florence. The next day he took them and the other notes he'd been taking to the Wayfarer and there, at a back table, continued to write furiously. The guilt-inflicted block he'd been fighting for two years had been broken, and the words were flooding out. It was a glorious feeling.

At the beginning of the third and final week they were to spend in Whitby, Stoker decided that scenes from the book would be set there and went to talk to the lighthousekeeper for a little while. He then went to the graveyard to listen to more of the old fisherman's stories.

"What is it tha be writin'?" Barnaby asked him.

"A novel" Stoker said.

"A novel?" Barnaby asked. "Make believe, is it?"

"Yes," Stoker said, "make believe, but with some basis in fact."

"And what would tha be usin'?" the man asked. "Our names?"

"No," Stoker said, "only places. The abbey, the graveyard, the beach . . . I'll be setting some scenes at night, so I should come out later, after dark. I want to see what the cliffs and the beach look like then."

Stoker looked down at his notes. That day it had been overcast, and so he wrote about how gray everything appeared . . . the clouds and the sea mist hanging over the ocean.

"Young fella," the old fisherman said, taking hold of Stoker's elbow, "let's be takin' a walk."

Stoker was about to protest, but the old man's grip was powerful and insistent. They began to walk away from the others, away from the graveyard toward the cliffs.

"What is it?" Stoker asked. "Is something wrong?"

"There's somethin' tha needs ta be warned about," the man said. "The others, they won't say nowt about it, but I think it's only fair tha knows."

"And what's that?"

The old man looked around to make sure no one else was within earshot.

"Tha doesn't want to be wanderin' around the graveyard at night," he finally said.

"And why not?"

" 'Tis haunted."

"By ghosts?"

"By them's be livin', and them's be dead," the old man said, "and them's caught in between."

"Is this a riddle?"

"It's a warnin'," the man said. "No more, no less. Open yer lugs and heed the warnin', is all I'm sayin'. I'll say nowt about it anymore."

"But wait," Stoker said, as the man started away. "Barnaby!"

But the old man kept walking and never turned back.

Later in the afternoon Stoker went to the Wayfarer for a pint. He drank it at the bar, so he could speak with the proprietor.

"Still takin' notes?" the man asked. Most of the men who frequented the pub were used to Stoker's manner.

"Yes," Stoker said, "being here in Whitby has inspired me."

"Don't get much readin' done these days," the man said. "This place keeps me pretty busy."

"Have you lived here long?" Stoker asked.

"All me life," the man said, and that looked to be fifty hard years or so.

"Then maybe I can ask you a question."

"Ask away," the man said. "I'll answer if I can."

"Somebody told me something today, and I was wondering if you could verify it."

"And what's that?"

"Something about St. Mary's graveyard being haunted."

He scowled and asked, "Is it Barnaby tha have been hearin' this from?"

"Well . . . as a matter of fact . . ."

"There are some stories," the proprietor said, "but nobody's really seen anything . . . except ol' Barnaby, or so he claims."

"What does he claim to have seen?"

"You can't be believin' everything ol' Barnaby says, now."

"I will keep that in mind."

The barman leaned his elbow on the bar and drew Stoker in closer.

"He claims to have seen a man in the graveyard, dressed all in black, doin' somethin' with the . . . the graves."

"Doing what?"

"Diggin' them up."

"And who's the man?"

"Barnaby claims he lives in a house up on the east cliff, and that he only comes out at night."

"Nobody else has ever seen him?"

"No."

"And is there a house where Barnaby says there is?"

"There's a fella lives in a house up there, keeps to himself all the time. Moved here some ten year ago or so. Never comes down to the village, never leaves his house during the day. Barnaby, he's the only one to have seen him at night."

"What about supplies? Food?"

"The bloke has them delivered. The delivery boy says he always leaves a box of supplies on the front steps."

"And he's never seen anything?"

"He doesn't want to!" the man said. "It scares the shite out of him to go up there."

"And no one else has attempted to talk to him?"

The man stood up straight and wiped the bar with a rag. "If the man wants privacy, we all say let him have it."

"Does he ever leave Whitby?"

"As a matter of fact," the man replied, "he was gone for a few months one summer . . . oh, musta been two years ago."

"The summer . . . of eighty-eight?"

"Now that you mention it," the proprietor said. "Someone said they saw him at the train station after dark, boardin' the late train to London. Yep, that musta been eighty-eight."

"London?" Stoker felt a coldness in the pit of his stomach, and his heart pounded in a way it had not since that night on the Thames ferry.

"Came back the same way, after dark, and ain't left since."

"And . . . he always wears black?"

"Black cloak, seems I heard Barnaby say once. You might ask down to the train station."

"I might just do that," Stoker said. "Thank you."

3

Stoker went back to the room and ate dinner with Florence. Afterward, they sat out on the balcony together.

"You are quiet tonight," she commented.

"I have a lot on my mind."

"Are we to return to London early?" she asked. "Are you thinking of the theater?"

"No," he said, "we will be returning the end of the week, as we planned."

"What is it, then?"

"The book." he said. "I have started making notes for the book."

She stared at him for a moment, then asked, "*That* book? After all this time?"

"Yes," he said, "that book." He stood, preparing

to leave. He did not want to hear what she had to say on the subject.

"Where are you going?" she demanded.

"For a walk."

"But it's getting dark."

He didn't reply, just picked up his jacket and left.

Stoker walked up the road to the East Cliff. He did not bother going to the train station to confirm the story he'd heard from the proprietor of the Wayfarer. Instead, he wanted to take a look at the house, although he had no idea of doing anything beyond that.

What if this was, indeed, Jack the Ripper? And what no one in London knew was that this Yorkshireman had one day decided to go to London and spend the summer killing women of ill repute and then return home, to what was apparently a hermit's life. As had been the case during the time Stoker had been Jack's confidant, he now knew something no one else did. Would it make any sense to tell someone? What would the local constabulary do if he did tell them?

He saw the house, silhouetted against a still gray sky. It was late enough that if he chose to walk all the way up the road to the door it would be dark by the time he knocked. What would he say to the man who answered the door? "Hello, Jack. Remember me?"

The thought chilled him to the bone, in spite of the fact that it was an August night. Or perhaps it was simply the sea breeze carrying the beginnings of a storm up the cliffs.

Indeed, why should he say anything to anyone? Jack's reign of terror had been over these past two years. The trip to Whitby had apparently expiated enough of Stoker's guilt that he had begun writing his book. Did he want to risk that by once again making the acquaintance of a mad killer?

There was a light on in the two-story frame house, on the second floor, and for a moment he thought he saw a figure in the window—a dark figure, looking out . . . right at him. For a moment it was as if they were staring right at each other—perhaps into each other's souls, if indeed the killer had one. In that instant Stoker knew that it was him, and then the figure moved away from the window, cutting short what was the last time Bram Stoker would ever lay eyes on Jack the Ripper.

Bibliography

Bram Stoker by Barbara Belford (Alfred A. Knopf)

The Crimes, Detection and Death of Jack The Ripper by Martin Fido (Barnes & Noble Books)

The Ultimate Jack the Ripper Companion by Stewart P. Evans & Keith Skinner (Carroll & Graf)

The Doctor and The Detective: A Biography of Sir Arthur Conan Doyle by Martin Booth (St. Martin's Press)

Teller of Tales: The Life of Arthur Conan Doyle by Daniel Stashower (Henry Holt)

THE SIXTH PHASE

ROBERT J. RANDISI

He is so careful and clever that at first the cops have bodies but no reason to link the murders, nothing to indicate that they are the gruesome handiwork of one man. But a combination of instinct, police work and luck leads one detective to suspect the truth—a truth so horrible that no one wants to believe it. But even as the terrifying reality becomes all too clear, there is still one question that no one can answer—why? What can possibly drive someone to commit acts so evil they sicken even seasoned police officers? As the police begin to understand the madman's twisted motives, they also begin to grasp the true horror of what has started the killing spree . . . and what they have to do to stop it.

___4651-2 $5.99 US/$6.99 CAN

Dorchester Publishing Co., Inc.
P.O. Box 6640
Wayne, PA 19087-8640

Please add $1.75 for shipping and handling for the first book and $.50 for each book thereafter. NY, NYC, and PA residents, please add appropriate sales tax. No cash, stamps, or C.O.D.s. All orders shipped within 6 weeks via postal service book rate. Canadian orders require $2.00 extra postage and must be paid in U.S. dollars through a U.S. banking facility.

Name_____
Address_____
City_____ State_____ Zip_____
I have enclosed $_____ in payment for the checked book(s).
Payment <u>must</u> accompany all orders. ☐ Please send a free catalog.
      CHECK OUT OUR WEBSITE! www.dorchesterpub.com

IN THE SHADOW OF THE ARCH

ROBERT J. RANDISI

Joe Keough, a former New York City police detective, moves to St. Louis to get away from the bloodshed of the Big Apple and start fresh. But five minutes into Keough's new life, four-year-old Brady Sanders walks into his St. Louis police station, leaving behind a trail of bloody footprints.

That is only the beginning of a twisted trail of darkness and fear, from Brady's missing parents and their blood soaked house, to the kidnapping of beautiful mothers and their small children. Are these hideous acts a series of unrelated coincidences, or is there a serial killer on the loose, stalking and killing the citizens of St. Louis? It isn't long before Keough is forced to realize that death in the Midwest is no different from death in New York. Terror is terror, no matter where you live.

___4761-6 $4.99 US/$5.99 CAN

Dorchester Publishing Co., Inc.
P.O. Box 6640
Wayne, PA 19087-8640

Please add $1.75 for shipping and handling for the first book and $.50 for each book thereafter. NY, NYC, and PA residents, please add appropriate sales tax. No cash, stamps, or C.O.D.s. All orders shipped within 6 weeks via postal service book rate. Canadian orders require $2.00 extra postage and must be paid in U.S. dollars through a U.S. banking facility.

Name_____

Address_____

City_____State_____Zip_____

I have enclosed $_____ in payment for the checked book(s).

Payment <u>must</u> accompany all orders. ☐ Please send a free catalog.

CHECK OUT OUR WEBSITE! www.dorchesterpub.com

ALONE WITH THE DEAD

ROBERT J. RANDISI

New York City is in the grip of a nightmare. A twisted serial killer called the Lover is stalking young women, leaving his calling card with their dead bodies—a single rose. And there's a copycat out there too, determined to do his idol one better. But the Lover isn't flattered. He's furious that some rank amateur is muddying his good name. As the nightmare grows ever more intense, one detective begins to suspect the truth. As his superiors close ranks on him, he realizes that his only ally may be the Lover himself.

___4435-8 $4.99 US/$5.99 CAN

Dorchester Publishing Co., Inc.
P.O. Box 6640
Wayne, PA 19087-8640

Please add $1.75 for shipping and handling for the first book and $.50 for each book thereafter. NY, NYC, and PA residents, please add appropriate sales tax. No cash, stamps, or C.O.D.s. All orders shipped within 6 weeks via postal service book rate. Canadian orders require $2.00 extra postage and must be paid in U.S. dollars through a U.S. banking facility.

Name_____

Address_____

City_____ State_____ Zip_____

I have enclosed $_____ in payment for the checked book(s).

Payment <u>must</u> accompany all orders. ❑ Please send a free catalog.

CHECK OUT OUR WEBSITE! www.dorchesterpub.com

SERVANTS
OF CHAOS
DON D'AMMASSA

The isolated little fishing village of Crayport, Massachusetts, might seem almost normal at first glance, but appearances can be deceiving. You would never be welcome there. Outsiders never are. The inhabitants of the village are unusually hostile toward strangers, and you might notice some of them share an odd physical trait. . . .

If you look very closely, though, you might discover the hideous secrets of the mysterious island off the coast. And if you aren't careful, you'll meet the powerful group that dominates the town, the ones known only as the Servants. Just pray you never catch a glimpse of the Servants' unimaginable masters.

Dorchester Publishing Co., Inc.
P.O. Box 6640   ___5069-2
Wayne, PA 19087-8640   **$5.99 US/$7.99 CAN**
Please add $2.50 for shipping and handling for the first book and $.75 for each book thereafter. NY and PA residents, please add appropriate sales tax. No cash, stamps, or C.O.D.s. Prices and availibility subject to change.
Canadian orders require $2.00 extra postage and must be paid in U.S. dollars through a U.S. banking facility.

Name _____
Address_____
City_____ State_____ Zip_____
E-mail_____
I have enclosed $_____ in payment for the checked book(s).
Payment <u>must</u> accompany all orders. ❏ Please send a free catalog.

CHECK OUT OUR WEBSITE! www.dorchesterpub.com

GERARD HOUARNER

ROAD TO HELL

Max is a man. An assassin, to be exact. But within him lurks the Beast, an unholy demon that drives Max to kill—and to commit acts even more hideous. Throughout the years, the Beast has taught Max well, and Max has become quite proficient in his chosen field. He is an assassin unlike any other. To put it mildly.

But now Max has a son, an unnatural offspring named Angel. Through Angel, the spirits of Max's former victims see a way to make Max suffer, to make him pay for his monstrous crimes. And while Angel battles his father's demons, Max himself must try to escape from the government agents intent on capturing him—dead or alive.

Dorchester Publishing Co., Inc.
P.O. Box 6640   ___5065-X
Wayne, PA 19087-8640   **$5.99 US/$7.99 CAN**
Please add $2.50 for shipping and handling for the first book and $.75 for each book thereafter. NY and PA residents, please add appropriate sales tax. No cash, stamps, or C.O.D.s. Prices and availibility subject to change.
Canadian orders require $2.00 extra postage and must be paid in U.S. dollars through a U.S. banking facility.

Name _____
Address_____
City_____ State_____ Zip_____
E-mail _____
I have enclosed $_____ in payment for the checked book(s).
Payment <u>must</u> accompany all orders. ❏ Please send a free catalog.

CHECK OUT OUR WEBSITE! www.dorchesterpub.com

ATTENTION
BOOK LOVERS!

Can't get enough
of your favorite HORROR?

Call **1-800-481-9191** to:

— order books —
— receive a **FREE** catalog —
— join our book clubs to **SAVE 20%**! —

Open Mon.-Fri. 10 AM-9 PM EST

Visit
www.dorchesterpub.com
for special offers and inside
information on the authors you love.

 We accept Visa, MasterCard or Discover®.